Trilogy of the Ghosts

By

Christopher Mercon

The Summer of the Ghosts (prologue)

Ghost Games

Ghosts Are People, Too

Tribulations of the Ghost

Trilogy of the Ghosts

© 2025 Christopher Mercon
All rights reserved

The author welcomes any comments, questions or inquiries regarding any of his stories, poetry. or any of his writings. He can be contacted by email at:
chrismercon@hotmail.com

Acknowledgements

The friends and supporters that made it possible to get this book published.

Jayn Baker   *   Jo Ann Troy   *   Eric Townsend

Author's Note:

The ghosts in this story communicate non-verbally; their communication is indicated by italics, not by quotation marks. As the people around them learn to and choose to communicate this way, their speech is also italicized. Very often, the people around them prefer to speak aloud.

Important definition:

Permeate: To pervade or diffuse throughout; to surround and fill; to spread through a space or every part of something.

Permeation: The act of surrounding and filling; the saturation of something; the assumption of something. (Assumption being the action of taking responsibility or control.)

Forward

By Raoul Tinsberg

When Jenny awakens to find herself in a hospital room, looking down at the body of a 14-year-old girl in a bed six feet below, she's confused and disoriented.

But when her high-spirited, best friend, Dolly (a ghost since the 1770's), shows up to reassure her that, although she was hit by a car while crossing to the school bus, she is still alive and the body, in a coma in the bed below, is indeed hers.

What do we do now? Jenny asks.

And so, begins a game, an adventure, a journey that involves more than either girl (or the reader) could ever imagine.

Some may claim to have been blindsided by this story that starts out as a harmless, young adult, coming-of-age whatever, that soon turns into a tale beyond genre—not quite sure if it is a ghost story, science fiction, spiritual, mystery, action/adventure, suspense thriller, romance or philosophy; but aside from genre, it is a stunning, hard-hitting, well-written collection that will challenge most people's beliefs and reality.

I've never read a book like this; of the thousands of books I've read in this long life, It's the first book I've ever read that should come with a warning label, because it will brilliantly, relentlessly, and unreasonably challenge everything you have ever assumed to be true and real.

Another caution: should you start reading this book at bedtime, you may find yourself still engrossed when the morning comes.

Yet it's just a story about two young girls, their unshakeable friendship and their amazing adventures...

R. T.

Table of Contents

Prologue

The Summer
of the Ghosts

By

Christopher Mercon

As published in *Storyteller,*
the Selected Writings of Christopher Mercon
© 2018 Christopher Mercon

Jenny was bored. There was nothing she really wanted to do, and she knew that if she spent much time in the house, her mother would find *something* for her to do.

It was a Saturday afternoon in the springtime. She had gone to ballet class that morning, so she didn't have to practice this afternoon though she didn't mind practice. Dancing was one of the things she really enjoyed and would do all the time if she could.

She wandered down the tree-lined street, past the white picket fence and a stone wall that was especially good for sitting on, but not right now.

Without really thinking about it, she headed toward the cemetery. Her mother didn't like her going there, but it was a cure for boredom. And her mother had never told her *specifically* not to go there.

New England had to have the best cemeteries anywhere. She noticed some of the headstones had dates going back as far as the Revolutionary War. One stone was her favorite, although it was very sad. The date of birth was June 9, 1884. The date of death was September 4, 1886. On the headstone was an inscription:

"Sleep here, child, and take thy rest,

God called you back, He thought it best."

There was more to the verse, but that part of the stone had been buried over time.

How could something be so sweet and yet so sad? she said to herself. *And how could those people be so brave when their baby died?*

It gave her an eerie but sadly sweet feeling to read the

stones of people who were all but forgotten. They had lived their lives right here in this city. *They walked down the same streets that I walk down yet in a different time.*

She tried to imagine how the city looked when some of these people lived. Somehow, she could imagine it: horse drawn carriages, pumps in people's kitchens, no electricity, and everyone crowded around the fireplace during winter. She could imagine them skating on the pond in the park the same way she did in the winter; that wouldn't change much.

She imagined that Christmas was better back then. She had seen *A Christmas Carol* at least once a year all her life, and it just seemed that was the way it should be! People dressed better. The men were more handsome, and they put their coats on puddles. The women would dress in full, beautiful gowns and go to affairs in carriages.

And the cemetery—she was sure that hadn't changed much.

The sun was setting, and that was the time when the cemetery was most beautiful: the green lawns and flowers everywhere! There were trees so big around that she imagined it would take five girls her size, hand in hand, to stretch around them. There were statues and pillars and the little stone houses they put people inside of instead of burying them.

She wondered why people sometimes made death so

beautiful and life so ugly.

*   *   *

In the twilight, the dancing couple seemed not out of place at all. She had a beautiful pink gown; he had long silver hair tied in the back, and short pants with a fancy jacket like she had seen in the movies. And they danced so beautifully!

They flowed across the lawn, their feet never touching the ground. With dancing like that, it seemed only natural. They danced and whirled, and the trees seemed to wave in unison. The cemetery was their ballroom, and it was all so perfect!

She sat enchanted for how long, she didn't know when suddenly it all vanished. She sat up, startled, and realized that it was dark out!

Oh boy, am I in trouble! she thought as she scurried home.

She arrived at the back door of her house, all out of breath. She stood on the back stoop, trying to suppress her heavy, telltale breathing. She saw her mother inside the kitchen and yelled, "I'm out here in the backyard if you need me."

"Where have you been?" her mother demanded. "Everyone else has already eaten! Come in here and eat your supper!"

*   *   *

Getting to the cemetery every evening wasn't easy. At first, she found it difficult to get out without her mother questioning her extensively. But she could always wear her down usually getting what she wanted, as long as she didn't do it too often.

The front gate to the graveyard was closed and locked every night at 5 p.m., but she could always get through the side gate that faced her street. They closed and latched it but obviously didn't feel the need to lock it.

Come, come, we haven't much time!

Jenny looked up, startled. He had appeared out of nowhere, dressed in some type of theater costume she was sure, but he didn't seem real. If the light were better, she might see right through him! And he was obviously talking to her.

"But I don't know you!" Jenny exclaimed.

I know you, he replied. *You're the little girl who comes here in the evenings and reads the names and dates on the tombstones.*

"I'm not a little girl, but I do read the tombstones. I almost feel like I know those people."

Why, then... you do know me.

"What?"

We must start the rehearsal.

"What rehearsal?"

Why, the evening rehearsal!

"For what?"

Why, the play. Now follow me!

She found herself following the man as he led her to a clearing in the center of the graveyard.

Where is she? he asked impatiently.

5

"Who?"

Why, Lady Marie. She plays the part of the spinster. You can play the part of the lady beggar.

She didn't think that sounded like a good part. And she wondered why, every time she asked him a question, his answers always started with the word *why*. He wandered off in the dimming light and returned with a woman she guessed to be about twenty years old. The woman was dressed in sandals and a gown with a belt around the waist and a top laced across her chest; obviously another costume. They were arguing about something. Jenny quietly crept over to listen; the woman didn't want to be in his play.

It was getting dark, and Jenny was getting nervous. Anxiously, she interrupted the quarrelsome couple. "I've got to go. I need to be home before the streetlights are on."

Now see what you've done, the man said to the woman. *There will be no rehearsal tonight!*

"I'm going!" Jenny said as she turned and fled the graveyard.

Passing through the gate, she left the world of costumed actors and dancers behind and found herself on the darkened sidewalk across the highway from her street. As she quietly pushed the gate closed, a man stepped out of the bushes and started toward her, scaring her quite a bit.

"Hey, little girl, come here," he said softly.

He was creepy, and she didn't like him; she was scared.

"I have to be home right away," she said, as she quickly turned and hurried toward her house.

She made it home okay and sat on the porch, shaking. She realized that people like that man were the reason her mother didn't want her out after dark. This was not going well at all. He was so creepy!

As she relaxed, she noticed how lovely the leaves of the tree in front of her house looked in the glow of the street-light. She sat gazing for some time at the golden light and the halo of illuminated leaves that it created. She wondered who those people in the graveyard were and why they would rehearse in the failing light.

"Jenny!" her mother called. She jumped up and quickly went inside.

"What are you doing out there this late?"

"I like it so much, sitting out there at night; the street light makes the tree look so pretty. Is it okay?"

"Well, if you ensure your homework is done before you go, I don't see any real harm in it."

*   *   *

There were two boys at school who went out of their way to tease Jenny. She especially didn't like the big one, Jeremy Smith. He had been held back a grade last year and seemed determined to make the kids in this grade pay for it, especially Jenny.

"I saw you sneaking into the graveyard last night, Jenny," he said snidely. "Is that to visit the other witches?"

The other boy was Eddie, a little redheaded kid whose nose always seemed to be running. Jenny could have knocked him down easily but he was brave when he was with his big buddy, Jeremy.

"Jenny the skinny!" Eddie chanted as she walked away from them.

*   *   *

I lost it in the big one.

As Jenny turned, she was startled to see a soldier leaning against the bench where she was sat. *Where did he come from?* she wondered. *People do seem to suddenly appear around here!*

"Who are you?" she asked. "And where did you come from?"

Sergeant John Remington, 4th Infantry, U.S. Army, he replied. *I lost it in the war.*

"Lost what?" she asked as she realized his left leg was missing from the knee down.

"Oh, I'm sorry!" she apologized.

Think nothing of it; I'm used to it by now, he said in a monotone.

"What war?" she asked.

The big one.

"What big one?"

The world war. The war to end all wars.

"Which world war?"

The big one, he replied.

She could see this was going nowhere. He wasn't even dressed like a real soldier; he looked like one from an old black-and-white movie. *Probably someone in another play,* she thought.

"Well, I must be going!" she said as she hurried on.

*   *   *

She saw two girls climbing a tree. *This is more like it,* she said to herself.

"Can I play with you?" she asked.

Of course! one of the girls replied. *My name is Amber, and this is Willow.*

"How do you get your mother to let you play out here this late?" she asked.

We don't have a mother, one of them replied.

Jenny was quite surprised by this. *Well, I guess that's how they're able to stay out this late. They must be sisters.*

"Doesn't your daddy make you come home when the streetlights go on?"

We don't have a daddy, the other girl said nonchalantly.

Oh, how awful! she thought, but it felt impolite to ask any further.

She realized it was getting late.

"Are you girls going to be here tomorrow afternoon?"

Of course! was their reply.

She was sitting on the front porch when her mother called her to come in for the night.

*   *   *

"Hi!" she said excitedly. "You two dance so beautifully! I watched the other night for the longest time, and it was enchanting. Do you think I could ever dance like that?"

Yes. We saw you the other night, the woman said. *We danced for you.*

"Why me?" she asked.

Because you take time to remember us. You read the stones and think of us.

"You're not real, are you?" she asked a little sadly.

Yes, we're real, the man said as he sat on the bench beside her. *We've just... passed on. And yes, you could dance like that someday.*

She stood. "You're ghosts?"

Oh, yes.

"All of you? The soldier, the actors, and the two girls?"

Yes.

"But why are you here?"

Everyone has to be somewhere, the man said.

The two actors appeared as she sat on the bench talking to the dancers.

"You're all ghosts! Wow! And I can never even tell my mom," she said wistfully.

But we never got to rehearse for the play, the actor griped.

"We can do that tomorrow night," Jenny said. "We can all be in the play the soldier, Amber and Willow, and you four. And me! This will be so exciting!"

"But now I've got to go; my mom will be expecting me."

*　　*　　*

Over the next several weeks, Jenny managed to get out almost every night. She was glad she had so many little sisters; her mother didn't have time to worry about her. She got used to Jenny going out after supper, sitting on the porch or playing in the yard.

Except she wasn't in the yard. She was at the graveyard with her friends; they put on plays. The actor's name was Mortimer; at one time he owned a theater about six blocks from her house, where he would put on plays every week. He claimed he'd still be there if they hadn't torn it down.

The dancers' names were Lance and Margaret. After much insisting, Lance agreed to teach her to dance. At first, Jenny felt awkward and self-conscious, but soon she found herself gracefully whirling about the lawn.

And she met more ghosts. There was an old woman named Millie who was afraid of Jenny and used to peek from behind a large tree. Jenny would wave and smile, but the old woman would vanish.

Then there was Malcolm, a huge Black man who used to work for the railroad. She loved to listen to him tell her stories of when "the railroad was king." Sitting back, listening to him talk about hobos and train wrecks and the endless miles of track he had traveled, she could picture everything. She favored him beyond the others.

One night she turned to him. "Malcolm, is the creepy guy a ghost?"

His face grew serious. *No, he's not a ghost. He's among the living but he's evil. You need to stay away from him. He hurts children.*

As time went on, more and more ghosts started showing up to be her friend. She didn't have time for any more ghosts! Enough is enough!

* * *

One night, as she was walking toward the graveyard, she noticed Jeremy and Eddie following her. She stopped and sat on the stone wall.

"Where are you going?" Jeremy demanded. "Are you going to the graveyard again?"

"It's none of your business where I'm going!" she scolded. "You should go away and leave me alone!"

"Maybe your mother would want to know where you go every night," he said.

"Don't you tell my mother anything! And don't you go near my house, either!" That would be a disaster if he opened his mouth; she really didn't like him.

Jeremy and Eddie continued to follow her. They thought she didn't see them but it wasn't hard. She went home.

* * *

The next day, she thought she saw Jeremy following her home from school. She went down an alley to double back and see. *This time I'll jump out screaming and scare him so badly he'll never bother me again.*

Seeing no sign of him, she turned to start back home then froze in her tracks. Partially hidden behind a fence was the creepy man, looking around. *He's trying to find where I have gone!*

Fear shot through her. This man scared her more than anything. She forced herself to start walking toward her house, trying to look unconcerned but struggling not to break into a crying, panicked run.

She finally got to her house, hurried up the front stairs, shut the door behind her and locked it. Trembling, she moved the curtain aside slightly so she could scan the street but saw no sign of the creepy man. *But I know he's out there!*

*   *   *

Jenny was determined to get to the graveyard that evening without Jeremy or the creepy man seeing her. What's more, she had to get home before her mother knew she was gone. Her nighttime adventures were getting difficult. She liked the people in the graveyard. She didn't like Jeremy, and the thought of the creepy man brought fear.

As she hurried across the graveyard toward the gate, she could see the streetlights across the highway come on one by one. As she turned to close the gate behind her, someone grabbed her arm! She had never been so scared— *the creepy man...*

But it was Jeremy!

"I want to know what you do in there!" he demanded.

Jenny's emotions flipped from terror to rage in a split second. She didn't bother pulling her arm away—she just slammed both hands into his chest, knocking him backward into some briar bushes. He started crying and screaming as he struggled to free himself. Jenny ran for home.

*   *   *

The next day, Jenny waited excitedly all afternoon for the sun to start going down so she could visit her friends at the graveyard.

Finally, sitting on the front porch, watching the sun drop toward the trees across the street, she decided it was time.

"Jenny!" her mother yelled.

Oh no! she thought. "Yeah?"

"I need you to go to the store and pick up some milk and a lemon."

"Oh, darn!" she muttered under her breath.

She ran to the store. The lemon bin was empty, which meant the shopkeeper had to get some from the back room but he was waiting on another customer. It was getting later and later, and she was getting so exasperated!

At last, he appeared with the lemons. She started to leave but he stopped her.

"Your mother called and said she needs some vanilla extract," he said, ambling across the store.

She finally had everything and left the store at a run. She was winded when she got to the house and put the bag on the counter.

"I'll be outside," she said to her mother, as she passed through the screen door and out onto the porch.

She ran all the way to the graveyard. Arriving out of breath and sweating, she eagerly pulled on the gate but it wouldn't move. It wasn't even latched! She pulled on it again, but despite her struggle, it wouldn't budge. There was no reason for that gate not to open.

Then something told her what it was: her friends didn't want her in there. She knew it as well as she had ever known anything. She felt it in the pit of her stomach—they didn't want her around.

She stood, staring up at the big wrought-iron gate, betrayal stinging her, squeezing grief from her stomach and chest. She turned and started walking toward home, tears slowly rolling down her face.

*   *   *

The next evening, she didn't know what to do with herself. She sat on the stone wall for a while, then started walking aimlessly; the graveyard loomed across the highway. The wind was playing games in the tops of the trees, and the grass had that freshly cut smell.

Well, I'll Walk by the graveyard, but I'm not going in!

She started down the sidewalk, keeping the highway between herself and the graveyard. As she got to the corner, she noticed some commotion at the front entrance, which was still open. She crossed the highway, stood by the main gate, and looked in.

There were three police cars, two fire trucks, and an ambulance; but no ghosts.

She walked through the entrance toward the police cars. There was no one around; then she saw the officers farther into the graveyard, standing behind a thicket of bushes by the far concrete wall.

She came up behind them unnoticed and stared in shock at the object of their attention. "Jeremy!" she screamed. They all turned, startled.

"You know this boy?" one of the officers asked.

"He's dead, isn't he! The creepy man killed him!" she screamed, crying and shaking. "The creepy man was following me, and Jeremy was following me, and the creepy man killed him!"

"Who is this creepy man?" a detective asked.

"I don't know! He's been following me!" she sobbed.

"I want you to come with me," he said gently. "We're going to go to your house to get your parents, then we're going to the police station. We're going to find out who this creepy man is."

It didn't take long for her to pick out his photo. The detective said he was a man known for bothering children. It was dark when Jenny and her mother left the police station.

*   *   *

Jenny found her mother sitting on the front porch swing. She snuggled between her mother's knees and leaned back as she felt her welcoming arms engulf her. She contentedly watched the sun go down.

"Jeremy used to pick on me, and he was mean but I'm sorry that happened to him," she said sadly.

"Yes, it is terrible when something like that happens," her mother said. "The police detective called this afternoon. He said the man they arrested confessed to killing Jeremy. It happened shortly after sundown; I don't know what Jeremy was doing in the graveyard at that time."

He was looking for me, she realized. *He was probably waiting inside for me to come, so he could find out what I was doing in there. But how could he get in? Oh, yeah, the ghosts didn't stop him...*

She made a sour face, then cried aloud, "Oh, my friends kept me from going in there so I wouldn't get hurt!"

She felt her eyes swell with tears of relief.

"They knew the creepy man was in there, and that he would hurt me. They're still my friends and they still love me!"

"What?" she asked. She was confused by Jenny's chatter.

"Oh, Mommy! I have to go find my friends!" she insisted, pulling out of her mother's arms.

"What friends? Where are you going?"

"Oh Mommy, I've got to go. Please, please, mommy! I've got to find my friends and thank them and tell them I love them and I'll always remember them!"

Her mother looked wary, but she had never seen her daughter so insistent.

"OK but don't be gone long! It's going to be dark soon, and I don't want you out after the streetlights come on!"

"OK!" Jenny yelled over her shoulder as she disappeared around the corner.

The End

Ghost Games

Trilogy of the Ghosts

Book One

By

Christopher Mercon

~ 1 ~

Dolly

Two years later.

The eerie whistling startled Jenny. It seemed to come from all around her; weird, unnatural howling. She had often heard reference to the whistling of the wind, but this was the first time she had actually heard it and it was creepy!

She closed the book and laid it on her desk, turned out the light and crawled across her bed to the window. In the darkness, the moon was big and round and yellow, the way it always was when it was just above the trees. Her mother said it looked that way because it was so close to the trees, but when it was way up in the sky, you had nothing to compare it to and the sky was so big. That made sense, but she preferred to think that some evenings just favored the moon.

Bare branches thrashed in the wind and leaves scattered in excited confusion. The cold of the autumn darkness seeped through the windowpane as she stared across the yard to the dark, empty lot next to her house. As her breath fogged a small circle on the glass, she was reminded that it was getting close to Halloween.

She turned and leaned back across the bed, reached over, and switched the desk lamp on. She pulled on her boots and took a sweater out of a drawer.

As she quietly moved down the stairs, she pulled the sweater over her head. By the time she closed the back door behind her, she had her jacket and poncho in hand. When she got the jacket on, she was relieved to find her gloves in the pockets.

The night was cold but comfortable; it felt good to breathe the crisp, clean air through her nostrils. She passed through the gate, closed it, then stopped to slip the wool poncho over her head.

She found herself walking faster than normal. The wind was glorious, setting all the darkened trees in motion. The night was alive and full of energy.

She enjoyed kicking her feet through the crunching leaves, making a loud rustling sound that she was sure could be heard all over the neighborhood but it just felt so good.

She loved the yellowed streetlights; just far enough apart that each created its own little island of light—each different from the others. The streetlights in the trees created a golden glow that turned the leaves around them into a gilded dandelion.

When she got away from the houses, she would sing. As she walked, she always found just the right song.

She was startled by footsteps! She had been so caught up in singing, and the wind, and the beauty of the streetlights that she had not seen or heard the man until he was almost in front of her. Her shoulders went tight with fear, and her singing abruptly ended as the words died in her throat.

He was very tall, and she felt tiny. He wore a ball cap that cast a shadow from the streetlight above, making his face a black hole. His boots scuffed loudly as he rapidly approached. She wanted to run but was petrified by fear. As he continued toward her, she thought of her mother.

Then he loomed above her.

"Good evening," he said softly as he passed by and continued down the street.

She said nothing but turned and watched as he passed out of the light and slowly faded into the darkness. She listened as the tap of his footsteps diminished. He appeared again in the cone of light below the next streetlamp, then disappeared into the night.

The magic was gone, as was her song replaced by thoughts of her mother and how she would explain being several blocks from home this late at night; she turned and hurried home.

*   *   *

She was breathing hard when she reached the front porch but didn't want to go right in. She was still uneasy about what had happened and felt stupid for being so scared. And she didn't want the fun she was having to end at least not like that.

She sat on the swing and pushed against the front railing of the porch with her foot, setting the swing in gentle motion. She pulled her knees up to her chest, lifting the poncho to cover them as she stared out at the night, willing the magic to return.

He wouldn't have scared me.

She turned to find Dolly sitting beside her.

I wasn't scared. He just startled me. Who was he?

Dolly shrugged her shoulders. *I don't know. What are you doing?*

Nothing. I was just out walking, Jenny replied.

She was relieved to see Dolly. She had met her at the graveyard almost two years ago. Jenny didn't have many close friends. She tended to be, as her mother would say, "in her own world." But she found so much of herself in Dolly that she wished they could be best friends forever. They were the same age, but Jenny was very aware that would change as time went on. Dolly would never get any older.

How did you find out where I lived?

Again, Dolly shrugged. *I don't know. I just wanted to find you and ended up here. Where have you been? We haven't seen you for two weeks!*

Well, Jenny said sadly, *it gets darker much earlier now and it's harder for me to get everything done and get out; and when I finally do, it's way after dark. This is the first night I've gotten out at all since I last saw you.* She turned to the ghost. *I didn't know you ever left the cemetery.*

Not often. The others seem to like it there and never leave, but sometimes I find it quite boring.

What about Willow and Amber? They're our age.

Yes, Dolly replied, *but they never want to do the things I wish to do. And I'm quite a bit older.*

Jenny was confused. *I thought you were my age. I'm the same age as them. Or I was two years ago when I first met them.*

No! I don't mean that..., Dolly said, shaking her head.

I was there long before they showed up. And it was two years before I could convince them they were ghosts!

How long have they been there? Jenny asked.

Twenty years, I would think.

And how long have you been there?

Quite a bit longer. I was alive before there were automobiles or any type of machines. I think America had just become a country when I was a girl. You lose track of time quite easily when there's a lot of it.

Hmm, Jenny said. *I never thought of that.*

It occurred to Jenny that they should find Dolly's gravestone sometime. She must have one there; that was the graveyard where they met. But it was considered poor etiquette among ghosts to ask about the past. If they wanted to tell you, they would.

She stared off into the night, thinking about Dolly being around that long and what she must have seen. *And she is only a little girl! Or is she?* Jenny got confused and stopped thinking about it.

Aren't you cold? Jenny asked. *You're only wearing that dress!*

I'm a ghost, silly! I don't really feel the temperature unless I pay attention to it and even then, it's not uncomfortable... I just sort of know it's cold.

Oh... Jenny's thoughts drifted.

Suddenly the overhead light blazed on, bathing the porch in the yellow glare of a bug light. Dolly was gone.

"What are you doing out here this late?" her mother demanded. "It's nine o'clock! Is your homework done?"

Jenny stood quickly. "Everything's done except for the book report, which doesn't have to be finished until Monday. I didn't know it was that late. I was just sitting out here."

"Well, inside! When you're going to be sitting out here, I want you to let me know where you are."

"Yes, Mommy," Jenny said as she swept past her mother and up the stairs to her room.

*   *   *

The next evening, Jenny was lying on her bed reading the book for her book report. Reading was fun, but then would come the hard part—writing the report. Maybe that would change after she finished the book.

Hi, what are you working on?

She looked up to see Dolly sitting in the chair by her desk.

A book—for a book report; but I don't mind it's really good.

Can you get out? Dolly asked.

Where's my mom?

She's doing dishes, Dolly replied.

I don't know... She looked over at the clock. It's only six-thirty, but it's dark outside...

When she got to the bottom of the stairs, she grabbed her jacket and poncho, and started getting dressed for the weather.

"I'm going to be outside," she yelled to her mother.

"Is all your homework done? What about that book report?"

"It's fine. The rest is done and I'll have the report finished by tomorrow night, early."

"Can you walk down and get me a gallon of milk? We'll need it in the morning, and I forgot to stop on my way home."

"Yeah," she said, trying not to sound too eager. Her mother approached from the kitchen, purse in hand, and handed Jenny a ten-dollar bill.

"I'm probably crazy sending a 14-year-old girl out after dark, but it's only six-thirty and I trust you. You go straight there and come right back. Don't go anywhere else."

"I'm fine," Jenny said as she headed out the door. She almost told her mom not to worry because Dolly would be with her. *Whoa, I've gotta watch that!*

Dolly was beside her before she reached the sidewalk.

Wow, Jenny said. *She never sends me out after dark!*

They walked together in silence. Jenny was excited to see Dolly again.

Hey, she said suddenly. *You're wearing a jacket! How come?*

I just thought you'd be more comfortable if I did.

Yeah, I guess I am. I didn't know you could change clothes. How do you do that?

I don't know, Dolly replied. *I just thought it would be good if I wore a jacket, and tonight I'm wearing one.*

Wow, Jenny said softly.

When she got into the store, she realized Dolly wasn't with her anymore. *Well, of course she's not going to follow me in here.*

As she left the store, Dolly was again by her side.

You remember what we were talking about last night? Jenny asked.

Yes... Dolly said, anticipating.

You said Amber and Willow didn't know they were ghosts...

Not for a while, Dolly replied. *Then one day, they just seemed to get it.*

Don't all ghosts know they're ghosts?

No, Dolly said. *There are a lot of ghosts who just wander around not knowing what's going on. I've met some very stupid ghosts.*

I haven't seen that many. Maybe three dozen? And I don't know any stupid ones.

Well, the stupid ones are afraid, and they're mostly in hiding, Dolly said. *A lot of them hide up in trees or behind bushes and they're sort of... not there.*

What do you mean, not there?

They just sort of... fade away, Dolly replied. *And then even I can't see them.*

When they got to Jenny's house, she went inside, put the milk in the fridge, and stashed the bag in the pantry.

"I need you inside now," her mother said, coming up behind her. "Martha has an emergency. I'm going across the street to stay with her toddlers for an hour. You stay with your sisters. I'm taking Dawn with me. The twins are already in bed and Wendy's downstairs watching TV. I'll be back before your bedtime. Martha's number is on the fridge. Call if there's any trouble. And I want you inside, not on the porch."

Jenny's stomach sank. She wanted to sit outside and talk with Dolly. Now she couldn't. She didn't even know if she could find her and explain.

Well, somehow, I think she'll know.

Dolly only showed up when Jenny was alone. Never when it would be difficult, and never in the house except her bedroom.

Soon, Jenny knew when Dolly was around without seeing her. She often wondered what Dolly did when they weren't together. She wanted to ask how she always knew where Jenny was but Dolly would just shrug and say she didn't know. And Jenny believed her.

Jenny's best friend was a ghost. And she was never lonely.

*   *   *

~ 2 ~

The Christmas Tree

Autumn turned into winter; early winter turned out to be one of the most severe in years. It was a season of snowplows, missed school days, and snow piled everywhere. As they walked to the school bus, Jenny watched heavy equipment load snow into dump trucks to be taken—where, Jenny couldn't imagine.

Skating on the pond wasn't possible; the ice was under several feet of snow and going to the graveyard was out of the question, but her friends would understand.

Still, not a day passed without Dolly appearing, at least for a little while. Jenny found it mysterious how Dolly always seemed to know when to come and when to stay away. If Dolly showed up while Jenny was struggling through homework, it would be too easy to get distracted and fall behind; that would be a disaster.

* * *

One night, Jenny turned off her light and sat on the floor in front of her bedroom window. She pulled her blanket around her shoulders and slid the window up. As the frigid air drifted into the room, she stared across the empty lot to the woods beyond. The moon hung low and frosty-white, resting just above the treetops. Its silvery light reflected off the freshly fallen snow and made the world seem like daylight.

Beautiful, isn't it? Dolly said, leaning on the window-sill. *Aren't you cold?*

No, Jenny said wistfully. *It's only for a few minutes... and it's so beautiful. Like a magic fairyland.*

Can we go out? Dolly asked.

Jenny checked the clock. Almost seven. It might be hard to explain to her mother why she wanted to sit outside on such a cold night but maybe if she showed her how beautiful it was...

Yeah, she said. *I'll meet you out there.*

Dolly appeared again as Jenny passed through the front gate.

Let's go to the woods, Jenny whispered, stepping into the lot.

But it wasn't completely empty there was one single pine tree in the center. Jenny always thought it looked lonely, standing there by itself. The whole scene seemed lonely.

Solitude, Dolly said. *Not really lonely.*

Jenny thought about that; *solitude isn't always a bad thing...*

They wandered through the snow-draped trees, spotting rabbit and squirrel tracks. Dolly said the bigger ones were from raccoons.

This is so beautiful, Dolly, Jenny whispered. *Everything is so shiny and bright, but it's dark out.*

Yes, Dolly said. *And the trees look so beautiful covered with snow.*

Jenny took Dolly's hand as they walked through the

magic forest.

We'd better get back; if your mother comes out and doesn't see you..., how would you explain that?

Oh, right, Jenny said. As they reached the edge of the lot, she was surprised to find just one set of footprints until she realized why.

* * *

Jenny sat at the supper table with her mother and younger sisters.

"I have an idea for Christmas," she said. "You know that pine tree in the lot beside the house?"

"Yes," her mother said, nodding her head.

Jenny explained her idea. After a moment of thought, her mother again nodded.

"Yes, that would be nice. I think we have everything you'll need."

That night, Jenny was in the empty lot, stringing lights on the tree while she and Dolly chatted. Jenny had to stand on a kitchen stool to reach the top branches; she ran an extension cord across the lot and plugged it into the side of the garage.

Later, she dragged her mother onto the porch.

Her mother gasped. "It's beautiful! The fact that it's all by itself makes it so special and everyone driving past the graveyard will see it."

That night, Jenny lay on her bed in the dark, staring out at the glistening tree. It sparkled like a multi-faceted star suspended in the December night sky.

That's really beautiful, Dolly said. *What a lovely idea. Sometimes you're so clever.*

Yeah..., Jenny said, hesitating as she spoke.

When we first saw it, it was shining in the moonlight and everything was perfect snow on the branches, no footprints. Now the snow's knocked off, there are dirty footprints everywhere, and the extension cord cuts across the lot like a scar. I just imagined it looking... prettier.

Yes, Dolly said. *I see what you mean.*

Two days later, Jenny had to take the late bus home from school. Snow had been falling all day but stopped just as she climbed onto the bus. She got off at the corner near the graveyard and turned then stopped and stared.

The Christmas tree stood in the center of the lot, its lights shining through a new layer of snow, soft and glowing. The extension cord was buried. No footprints.

It looked like something from a Christmas card; the most beautiful thing she had ever seen.

*   *   *

~ 3 ~

Coma

Spring finally arrived. Almost overnight, the world changed from icy streets and frozen ponds to melting snow, puddles, and splashing cars. Sometimes the roads became streams.

But this meant more time outside for Jenny. The days were growing longer again.

She saw the bus coming toward the graveyard entrance. As she reached the end of her driveway, the driver turned on the red flashing lights and stopped.

Jenny hurried across the highway, going around a puddle too wide to jump. She was about to leap over a smaller one when someone yelled.

As she turned toward the sound, a large blue car struck her, slamming her into the air. She landed face-down in a puddle and didn't move.

*   *   *

Awareness. Whiteness. Light... then dark; then light again.

Nothing to hold on to. Just there.

Trees waved slowly in the wind. Interesting. Time existed, but not here. There was only stillness. Light and dark. Light and dark.

A room with white ceilings. Of course, rooms always

had white ceilings. Curtains were light blue. The blanket, dark blue. People came and went—nurses, doctors; but they never spoke to the girl who wasn't there.

Her mother did. She read aloud and talked about Jenny's sisters and how much they missed her.

The girl in the bed never moved. One side of her head was bandaged. One leg was in a cast, suspended by cables. The other leg lay beneath the covers. One arm was casted too. Jenny watched her watch herself.

* * *

Jenny?

Huh?

Jenny?

Dolly? Is that you

Yes. How are you?

I guess I'm okay.

Do you know where you are?

No... Who is she?

That's you.

Jenny stared at the girl in the bed. She hadn't wanted to admit it, but now she felt the grief crashing in.

Dolly?

Yes?

What happened? Am I dead?

No. If you were, they wouldn't keep your body here. They'd bury it.

Nothing was said for a while.

Dolly?

Yes?

I guess I'm hurt... and not awake.

You've been in a coma since they brought you here.

When was that?

I don't know; a few weeks ago.

But how can I be up here, looking down at me?

Dolly shrugged.

*   *   *

Jenny began to understand why time didn't matter to Dolly. It just... didn't. Maybe a few weeks had passed. Maybe longer. It didn't seem to matter.

At first, Jenny was afraid, especially when strangers came in. But when her mother visited, held her hand, talked to her, she felt safe.

She watched the city from the window; she watched mornings where her mother asked the nurse to open the window for air.

And Dolly was always there. All Jenny had to do was think about her and she would appear. At first Jenny thought Dolly came because she was worried but then she realized: Dolly just wanted to be with her best friend.

*   *   *

You look different now, Jenny said.

Oh?

Yeah. Before the accident, you were a girl with dark hair, a little over five feet tall. You wore that full, pretty dress. But now... you're a mist. Sometimes just arms, shoulders, or a smile. Sunlight shines through you. In the dark, you glow dim and warm. You're like the opposite of a shadow.

Yes..., Dolly said, hesitating.

What? Jenny asked.

Come with me.

They appeared in the bathroom in front of the mirror. Jenny saw Dolly's reflection soft and glowing. Then her own; barely there. Gray, faint.

Oh no! You're so beautiful and I'm... plain. I don't like this.

You have to create it, Dolly said. *What do you want to look like?*

I want to shine like you do. You're so pretty.

You're beautiful too, Jenny.

No... I mean, my body is beautiful, she said, gesturing toward the hospital bed. *But this me is not,* as she gestured toward the mirror.

I've had practice, Dolly said. *You could see me before because I created an image. Remember how I disappeared when others came? Sometimes I didn't leave, I just stopped showing myself. Ghosts are invisible unless we create a form. Some ghosts can't control it. Others scare people. Sad ghosts wail; angry ones growl. It gives us all a bad name.*

Oh... So how can I make myself pretty?

You decide what you want to look like, Dolly said. *Picture it in your mind.*

I want that glow you have; like light shining through you.

35

Picture it. Now decide that is you.

Jenny watched her reflection. A soft glow appeared white, then shifting to silvery blue.

Oooh...

You did it! Dolly said. *Now try changing your face.*

Jenny focused, and her features became clearer.

Careful with glowing eyes, Dolly said. *They're easy to overdo you don't want to look like a ghoul.*

What's a ghoul?

Crazy ghosts. Angry ones. They make people feel terrified, even when invisible.

Creepy, Jenny said.

They are. But you can practice. Light affects how you look. Gaslight is prettier than LED streetlights. Candlelight is softest of all.

Neat, Jenny said.

Emotion changes it, too, Dolly added. *Happiness is white-yellow. Anger goes red. Crying? Grayish-black and definitely not pretty. But it depends on the kind of crying.*

I'm going to learn how to make myself really pretty.

Just remember, Dolly said seriously, *don't do it when people are around. They'll see you.*

* * *

~ 4 ~

The World Outside

It was a beautiful spring morning; the sun was shining and the sky was heavy with lush, full clouds.

Dolly had been trying to convince Jenny that they should, or that they could, go outside. Jenny didn't want to leave her injured body alone.

OK, then try this: just go outside the window, just a few inches. You can be outside and observe your body through the window.

Jenny looked at Dolly hesitantly.

How?

What do you mean?

How do you do it? Jenny wondered aloud.

Go outside? Dolly asked.

Yeah.

You just... Dolly hesitated. It was second nature to her. *You just be there...*

With Jenny's confusion increasing, Dolly continued. *Just look in through the window...*

What? Jenny asked.

Look in through the window! Dolly insisted.

But I... Suddenly Jenny was out in the bright sunshine, looking through the window at her body in the bed.

See? It's fine, Dolly said.

*　　*　　*

The next day, Dolly and Jenny were back outside the window of the hospital room.

There is so much motion in the city, Jenny thought. Below them, cars honked their horns and buses rumbled by. On the sidewalks, throngs of people crisscrossed, hurrying in a hundred different directions. The trees waved in the wind and bicycles rolled through the park. Jet planes and an occasional helicopter seemed to dot the sky.

You've been working on your image, Dolly said. *You are beautiful.*

Yeah, Jenny said, with an embarrassed grin. *I like it.*

Let's go up on the roof, Dolly said.

Jenny glanced through the window. The body seemed to be sleeping comfortably, but she didn't want to leave her alone.

Why don't we wait until my mother shows up?

Because you would never leave if your mother was here. Where could a body be safer than a hospital? She'll be fine. Come.

Jenny hesitated.

Look, we'll just go up to the roof for a few minutes and look around, then we'll come right back. It's a beautiful view. We should only be gone for two minutes.

Again, Jenny glanced through the window at the body that hadn't moved since it had arrived at the hospital.

OK, for a few minutes.

When they got to the roof, Jenny gasped. *This is so beautiful!*

The bright sun hung in the sky far above them and everything was so perfect. The blue ocean shimmered to the east of them. Below, the urban neighborhoods stretched south to infinity. The mountains to the north and west were layered in a spectrum of blue shades, going from darker to lighter.

*   *   *

Dolly, how come I can see?

What do you mean?

I don't have any eyes; I mean not that I can use. So, I'm not using my eyes, how come I can see? Actually, I can see much better now.

I don't have any eyes, either, Dolly replied. *I don't know how I can see. I never even thought about it.*

Yeah, but you're a ghost... Jenny said.

So, what's the difference?

What do you mean? Jenny asked.

I don't have a body. You're not using your body; you might as well not have one.

What do you mean? Jenny said, starting to sound concerned.

I mean right now neither of us have bodies, really. I don't have one. You have one but you can't use it. So, we're in the same sort of situation, don't you think?

Well... yeah. But that doesn't explain how I can see, Jenny said, avoiding the subject.

There must be some other way to see when you don't have eyes to see with.

Well, how come blind people can't see, then?

I don't know, maybe they're still trying to use their eyes to see.

Wow..., came Jenny's whispered reply.

*   *   *

Very soon, Jenny was able to recognize most of the pigeons that would arrive every morning to land on the roof. Somehow, they were aware of Jenny and Dolly and would get excited when the girls arrived. They weren't all regular dark-gray pigeons some of them were unique colors. There was a pretty dark red one that she figured was once tame, maybe a homing pigeon that couldn't find its home.

There were days when jet planes taking off and landing at Logan Airport seemed to pass right over them; they were magnificent, shining in the sunlight. She most enjoyed when they would turn above them and head east over the ocean; she would watch as they got smaller until they vanished.

*   *   *

~ 5 ~

Ghost Games

As dark clouds gathered and rain ensued, Jenny slipped back into the room.

Where are you going? Dolly asked.

Inside; it's raining.

So? Are you afraid of getting wet?

Well, I...

No! You can't get wet. Rain can be the most fun. You should enjoy the rain! Come with me, Dolly said as she headed into the sky.

Then they were several thousand feet up, unaffected by the deluge, engulfed by turbulent, rolling clouds and swirling sheets of rain.

Find a raindrop, a single raindrop, Dolly said.

Jenny found one, but it slipped away and plunged toward the earth below.

Embrace it! Dolly said excitedly, *lock onto it and hold on!*

Jenny captured a single raindrop; as it plummeted, she was on a dizzying ride as the ground rushed up at her. As she closed with the earth, she fled the raindrop and found herself back in the storm with Dolly.

It was going to smash into the ground, she said.

Let's go out over the ocean, Dolly replied.

Suddenly, they were out to sea. Staring through the

swirling rain, she could see tall city buildings a few miles to the west.

Grab another and hold on all the way down, Dolly said as she latched onto a raindrop and vanished.

Jenny found another, and with dizzying speed she plummeted. With an exciting splash, she plunged into the water and seemed to explode in all directions. A moment later, she was back in the clouds with Dolly.

That was amazing! Jenny said, laughing excitedly.

This time, go to the center of the raindrop and do it again, Dolly said.

I would have to be tiny! Jenny insisted.

Easiest thing. Just realize that you're tiny and look around to discover that you're in the center of the rain-drop; or just make the raindrop huge.

Huge?

Yes. Just make it bigger than you are.

Jenny focused on a single raindrop. Suddenly, she was underwater! She popped back to where Dolly hovered.

What was... I was underwater!

You were inside the raindrop! Where do you think you would be? The raindrop is full of water. If you go inside, you're going to be underwater.

As Jenny focused on another raindrop, Dolly spoke; *And stay inside!*

Suddenly she was looking at the world from inside the raindrop, underwater. Colors rushed by as she plummet-ed. As they smashed into the ocean's surface, the impact burst the raindrop in all directions, and with an intense rush of pleasure, Jenny burst with it.

Wow! she exclaimed.

Then she was back with Dolly, who hovered in the cloud with her laughing, magical smile.

More! Dolly said as she grabbed another raindrop and was gone.

Jenny found that she could control the downward trajectory and soon she was steering the raindrops as they plunged. As she sought out the biggest raindrops, she realized that by smashing one raindrop into another and then another, she could create much larger ones, which created intensely pleasant explosions when they hit.

Jenny spotted a fat raindrop. *Yes!*

When she popped inside the raindrop, Dolly was in there! Laughing and smiling, the two of them shared a raindrop, giggling gleefully all the way to the water's surface.

Wooooh! Dolly! This is the most fun I've ever had! she said, laughing.

All too soon the storm passed, leaving a huge rainbow and the joyful music of two laughing angels.

*   *   *

Jenny and Dolly were in the air about a thousand feet above the hospital. The lights of the city that stretched into the distance, abruptly ended at the water's edge, but for a few scattered over the ocean. To the southeast, the lights of Cape Cod extended away from the mainland.

The city was never quiet; there were always the sounds of automobile horns, factories busy on the night shift, aircraft taking off and landing, and subways clattering through the night when they came above ground.

Jenny knew the city quite well, geographically, but she didn't know the names of various places. She knew a few names from signs like Back Bay Bookstore or Beacon Hill Dry Cleaners but those were rare. It was amazing how many places in the city had no signs at all.

What are those? she asked, pointing at isolated lights in the darkness. They had no hands to point with, but she only had to focus her attention and Dolly would know what she meant. She could easily follow Dolly's focus to what she was talking about.

Some of them are islands, some are peninsulas and some are ships at sea. You can see the lights on the bridges that reach out to the islands...

Suddenly there was a roar that would have deafened them if they had ears. In an instant, they found themselves in a well-lit room full of people, all comfortably sitting in chairs arranged in rows. Some were reading books, some were staring into their phones or tapping on keyboards.

Then, just as quickly, they were back in the sky, looking down at the city below them. As she spotted a jet pulling away, Jenny realized what had happened.

What was that!?? Dolly demanded. *What just happened!?* She went from bewilderment to irritation at Jenny's gleeful laughter.

We just got hit by an airplane, silly! We were sitting in its path and it passed right through us or we passed through it. I'm not sure which.

What? Dolly asked.

Yes! It passed right through the exact spot where we were sitting. And so, for a brief moment, we were actually inside the airplane.

Oooh..., Dolly said.

And then we were out, Jenny continued.

They hovered in the sky, watching the lights of the plane as it got smaller, heading west.

*   *   *

It was another sunny afternoon with clouds, traffic, and the boisterous city stretching out below them.

Oh, my mom's here, Jenny said, and disappeared inside.

A moment later Dolly was beside Jenny. Their attention was on her mother who was sitting in the chair beside the bed.

"Well, Jenny," her mother said, "I think I have a good one today. I started going to the library on the east side. They have a whole different assortment of books."

When she pulled a book out of her purse and started reading, the two younger girls found their comfortable, familiar position on the end of the bed and put their attention on their mother.

Jenny and Dolly loved listening to her mother read stories. All the while Jenny was in the hospital; they never missed story time. At first, it made Dolly sad to think she didn't have a mother. Jenny stubbornly insisted that since they had agreed to be sisters as well as best friends, Janice was now her mom, at which point, her sadness seemed to dissipate.

The story today was about an ant named Albert who had difficulty learning to read. Jenny's mind drifted off to ant colonies with hundreds of rooms and thousands of ants. Having that many ants, they needed hundreds of rooms.

Just think of how many schoolrooms they needed! Dolly smiled as she followed Jenny's thoughts.

Wow, Dolly said. *We only see the entrance to the colony, but there's a whole city below the ground. And each ant entrance is another whole colony.*

*   *   *

Sunrise found Dolly and Jenny on the roof playing with the pigeons. The flock had grown; there were probably fifty this morning. Every so often, the flock would suddenly take off and fly in a huge circle around the building, way out, several blocks away. They moved as a single unit, the same way schools of fish swim. Then just as suddenly, they would return and settle onto the roof.

The pigeons would get a little anxious just before they took off. This time Jenny looked at Dolly and thought, *Let's go with them!*

As the flock lifted from the roof, the two girls joined. At first, it was a struggle to match the sudden turns and dips, but soon both girls were moving like seasoned members of the flock.

Suddenly Dolly stopped, causing Jenny to stop as the flock left them behind.

Listen, Dolly whispered.

Jenny heard nothing.

What?

How do you hear what I'm saying? Dolly asked.

I don't... Jenny stuttered. *There's a word for it, a big word.*

Perceive? Dolly asked.

Yes! How did you even know that word?

Dolly shrugged. It just came to me. I think I saw it in your mind. Great word.

Yes. I perceive what you say or think, actually.

Good. Do you 'listen'? Dolly asked.

I guess, Jenny said. *I think it's the same way I can see without eyes. I just... perceive it.*

So how do the birds know where to go? Dolly asked.

Jenny just looked at her.

I think they listen.

To who?

To each other? To the flock? I don't know, Dolly said, *but I think they listen. How else would they know?*

Wow, Jenny said.

We have to listen. Come! Dolly said as they returned to the flock.

Whoa!! Jenny said. *I hear it. It's a thought it's an instant thought.*

Yes, and you don't think with it. You don't have time. You just do it!

Oh my gosh, yes! Jenny said as they both instantly turned with the flock.

They felt a sudden rush of energy flow through themselves as well as the flock.

They know that we get it, said Jenny excitedly.

This is great, said Dolly.

The flock began flying in huge, joyous circles, doing intricate maneuvers that the girls followed flawlessly. They never imagined they would ever see a flock of birds laugh and smile.

*   *   *

Jenny and Dolly were on the roof watching the sun sink toward the horizon.

I want to go see Malcolm, Jenny said.

Oh? Dolly replied.

Yeah, I miss him. He was my best friend in the grave-yard before I found you.

Now? Dolly asked.

Yeah, Jenny said.

A moment later, the graveyard appeared below them.

He hangs out over there by those monu-ments, Jenny said.

I know, Dolly replied. I live here.

Then they were in front of Malcolm.

Malcolm? Jenny said to the startled ghost.

No! he cried. *No! Jenny, how did this happen?*

What? Jenny asked.

Malcolm looked at her very sadly, very distraught.

How did you die? he asked. *I haven't seen you for a while, but I never thought...*

No! Malcolm, she said. *I'm not dead!*

He looked even more surprised.

Then how...

She's in a coma, Dolly said.

A coma? I didn't know that could...

Yeah, I'm not dead!

Are you sure? asked Malcolm. *Sometimes people die and they don't know...*

Come, Dolly said as she reached toward Malcolm.

A moment later the three of them hovered outside the hospital window.

That's me, Jenny announced. *I've been there for a couple of months now.*

Wow, Malcolm said. *I believe you. But let's go back to the graveyard. I'm too much in the open here. I'm not used to this.*

When they were back at Malcolm's bench, he spoke. *What happened?*

I was crossing the street to the school bus and I got hit by a car—right over there, she said, pointing.

I've never heard of that before, Malcolm mused. *Somebody going into a coma and becoming a ghost.*

I'm a ghost? she asked.

Well, you're here, aren't you? Dolly said.

Yes, I'm here, but I'm alive, she insisted.

But you're still a ghost, said Dolly.

What's going to happen? Malcolm asked.

I don't know... she said.

Well, how long can your body last like that? he asked.

I don't know, she said, but his question gave her a funny feeling in her stomach or where her stomach would have been when she had her body.

*   *   *

Jenny and Dolly were seldom in the hospital room unless her mother was there, which was every afternoon. But this was early morning; they had plenty of time before she arrived.

I'm thinking about ants, Jenny said.

What about them? Dolly asked.

I want to go see ants, Jenny said.

What kind? Red ants? Army ants? Black ants? Tiny ants? There are even ants that are half red and half black.

Jenny's eyes widened. *Wow, really?*

Oh yes, Dolly said. *Come.*

Below them were several anthills swarming with big ants; they all had black heads and bottoms, but the center of their bodies was red.

Wow, Jenny said as they watched hundreds of ants running around. *This is so confusing! What do we do?*

Well, said Dolly, *we should probably pick one ant and follow him around.*

We could ride 'em, Jenny said.

I think we could actually permeate them, Dolly replied.

Permeate... that's another of your words... Jenny said.

It means to fill something and be around and inside of... like if smoke permeated your house. It's inside of it, and fills it, and is even outside of it.

Oh, I get it. It's like when something stinks, it perme-

ates the air.

Yes, that's it.

How... Jenny started to ask, then stopped. *You just realize you are permeating him.*

Yes! said Dolly, smiling.

Suddenly Jenny enveloped the ant as it quickly trotted along, its six legs moving like a machine.

Wow, this is—

Remarkable! Dolly said. *I've never done this...*

Well, I guess we just settle in and go along for the ride.

It was like the best amusement park ride as their vehicle quickly trotted through tunnel after tunnel, suddenly turning one way and then the other. The girls had to constantly switch ants to stay together.

Jenny was thrilled with the ant colony. Everyone was so busy! As they switched from ant to ant, she realized that everyone had their own job and they knew just what to do. And they just did it.

Then the tunnel widened as they passed into a huge chamber, filled with hundreds of ants.

This is the queen's chamber, Dolly said.

They watched as she deliberately deposited one egg after another.

She's huge, Jenny said. *I thought she'd be big and fat, but she's shaped like a regular ant, just bigger.*

They're a serious lot, Dolly said. *I don't think there is such a thing as a happy ant.*

Yeah, but they're not unhappy either, Jenny said.

How do they know what to do and where to go?

Dolly asked. *I haven't seen any bosses. Who tells the ants what to do?*

I don't know, Jenny said. *Maybe if we just listen...*

She got a shocked look on her face.

Oh my gosh, I don't believe it.

What? Dolly demanded.

Just listen really carefully. Do you get that? Jenny asked.

What is it? It's weird, Dolly said.

Jenny looked at her intently. *They all... they all have the same mind! There's only one mind directing everything!*

Dolly got a probing look on her face.

Oh! It's like... Dolly struggled for words. *Yes, they do... I thought they would each have their own mind, but it's just one!*

They're all like little robots, all being directed by one big computer, Jenny said.

I don't know about that, Dolly said. *Maybe they all just combined into one mind. It would be easier like that. But I think I get what you mean. That was the same thing with the flock of pigeons that's what we were listening to. They were all being directed by one mind, and we were listening to that mind.*

Jenny got a startled look on her face.

What? Dolly asked.

They..., that is weird... Jenny's words trailed off.

What? Dolly demanded.

The colony..., the ant colony—they are the mind!

What?

Yes! Jenny said. *It's the same with the flock of pigeons. The flock IS the mind! It's... it's a collective intelligence or awareness or consciousness or whatever.*

You mean... Dolly's words trailed off as she grasped the concept. *Oh..., I get it.*

Dolly looked over at Jenny and saw the same sense of wonder on her face that she was feeling.

*   *   *

~ 6 ~

The Responsibilities of
Living and Dying

The morning was passing into the afternoon as her mother got up to leave. As she directed the twins into the corridor ahead of her, she turned back toward the bed-ridden figure.

"Goodbye, sweetheart," she whispered.

Jenny reacted to the voice that spoke to her mother as she passed into the corridor.

Who is it? Dolly asked.

It's the Wicked Witch of the West, Jenny said. *It's my Aunt Agnes.*

The two girls followed the conversation as it moved toward the front of the hospital.

"I know what is best in situations like this," Agnes said. "When my Henry had his heart attack, we eventually took him off life support, and everyone was better for it."

"No!" Jenny's mother snapped. "Henry was brain dead. Jenny is not! I know she'll come back to me!"

"Well, I'm only trying to do what's best for you and the children."

Agnes was still talking as they turned a corner and passed out of sight.

Jenny was shocked. *Take me off life support? Does*

that mean I'll die? She's a terrible old woman! My mother would never do that!

Dolly said nothing as Jenny stood beside the bed and just stared off.

After a moment, Dolly spoke. *I'll be around if you need me,* then disappeared.

*   *   *

Jenny sat with Malcolm watching the sun disappear beyond the distant hills; dusk had arrived.

It's time, Malcolm, Dolly said.

Then they were standing beside a switch on a lonely stretch of railroad tracks; Malcolm had a signal lantern in his hand. Jenny recognized the distant rumble as an approaching train. As the sound grew louder, she could make out the figure of an antique locomotive moving toward them. Malcolm reached down, took hold of the switch lever, and pulled. The tracks shifted to allow the oncoming train to continue onto the rail in front of them. He stood tall, waving the yellow lantern over his head as the locomotive approached.

Jenny realized the train and the tracks were not real; it was as much a ghost as they were. Nonetheless, it roared by them as Malcolm continued waving the lantern. When it was passed, Malcolm grabbed the lever and switched the tracks back into their original position.

They watched the apparition grow smaller as it receded into the night. They could hear it long after it was out of sight and then the sound, too, vanished.

*   *   *

Jenny and Dolly were back at Malcolm's bench in the graveyard. Jenny was telling him about what her aunt had said to her mother. Dolly vanished when she realized Jenny wanted to be alone with Malcolm.

It is upsetting and scary, Jenny said. *I'm afraid and I don't know what to do.*

Well, what should happen? Malcolm asked.

I don't know..., she mumbled.

Whose body, is it? he asked.

Mine...

Then who should decide what happens to it?

Me... I guess. She was having a hard time with this.

What's going to happen with the body if you do nothing?

I don't know.

Well, it can't live forever, Malcolm said. *And from what you told me, it's not getting better. I know this is not easy, but I think you should make a decision. If you do nothing, the body will probably die.*

Jenny's stomach twisted as she spoke.

I don't want that! My mother would cry and be unhappy, and my sisters would cry. They'd all be unhappy. Why do I have to decide?

It's your body, Malcolm said grimly. *It's your responsibility.*

I've heard that word so often, Jenny said. *I don't even know what it means.*

That's when you own something and do the right thing for it, Malcolm said. *Or not.*

My mom says that I have to take responsibility for my little sisters, but I don't own them. She does.

Yet, you refer to them as <u>your</u> little sisters, Malcolm replied. *There are different kinds of ownership. Very often, people think that ownership is the need to possess things to take them and keep them and put them away somewhere so it only belongs to them. Until they die, and it stays behind, and they feel they've lost everything. That's why ghosts haunt houses; they're still trying to own the houses they once lived in.*

But you could own this graveyard, Malcolm continued. *Or you could own a beautiful day. You could even own a tree. It doesn't mean that I couldn't own that tree also. You see that big bright star up there above the tree?*

Yeah, she said.

What if you and I decided, right here, that was your star? Malcolm said. *We could even give it a name; we could call it Jenny's Hope. And when you need hope, you could find your star.*

She looked up at the star and then looked over at him.

What could you do to make it your star? he asked. *We've already given it your name.*

She looked up at him questioningly.

You just have to decide, really decide that it's your star, he said. *There's not even the slightest chance that anyone would doubt that it's yours. They would just know. And some other little girl could look at that star and maybe hope for something, and she would be making it her star. And that would be okay, because it would still be your star.*

Is that like wishing on a star? she asked.

Very much so.

Wow..., Jenny said, staring off into the night. *I could make anything mine, I guess.*

Yes! Malcolm said. *How about little sisters?*

Yes. They could be my little sisters.

What could you do for your little sisters now that they are yours?

I could make them happy, Jenny said. *I could read them stories. I could help them with their homework.*

Could you teach them how to be good girls? Girls that would grow up so you could be proud of them?

Yes, Jenny said. *That would be so good.*

They sat quietly, looking off into the dark. The sound of heavy footsteps intruded into her thoughts. As they got louder, she spotted a large man walking past the grave-yard. As he got further away, the sound grew softer and then was gone.

Do you think he was whistling? asked Malcolm.

Huh? she asked, but he said nothing.

It's quite a burden for a little girl, I know, Malcolm said after a moment, *but no one can tell you what to do, really.*

If I died, Dolly and I could just go on playing forever, Jenny said. *We have a lot of fun! We do all sorts of amazing things together.*

Malcolm said nothing as they sat, watching the skies

darken over the distant line of tree.

* * *

Her mother was sitting by the side of the bed. Jenny could see extreme worry and sadness in her eyes. She surrounded her mother and held her. This was permeation in the fullest sense of the word. She could feel her mother's emotions as her own; she could see her mother's thoughts. They were drifting back in time into memories of when Jenny was younger. Her first day of school, first grade; she was so proud of her new white dress. Her mother stood on the sidewalk watching as she bravely walked up the path. She looked back, waved, and went on into the school.

She wandered through the melancholy of her mother's memories—birthday parties, beach days, and quiet times when she was held in her mother's lap. Suddenly, the pictures whisked away and her sadness seemed to vanish.

Her mother stood, startling Jenny. She looked down at the figure in the bed and said goodbye, guided her two daughters ahead of her, and left the room.

* * *

Jenny found herself in a dark, dusty place she recognized as the top of the hospital air conditioning duct. She didn't want to be outside she didn't want to talk to Dolly. She didn't want to be alive, but neither did she want to be a ghost. She didn't know a ghost could be overwhelmed by such painful grief, but she was. She pushed herself into the darkest part of the duct and clung to the corner, trembling.

I'm so bad! I am hurting my mommy! Every moment I'm out here, I'm making my mommy so unhappy! I am bad for my mommy! I'm bad for everyone.

She had no idea how long she hid in that dark place. She knew that if she wanted Dolly to be there, she would be.

*   *   *

Heavy rainclouds rolled in above them as they hesitated on the edge of the roof.

Do you want to play in the rain? Dolly asked.

Jenny dismissed the idea with a frustrated shake of her head.

I don't know what to tell you, Dolly said sadly. *Malcolm seems to understand these things. I don't. To me, you're a ghost. You don't seem to be any different than any of the other ghosts I know.*

I have a body, Jenny said. *It seems that it is my responsibility and I don't know what to do!*

She thought about the aunt she feared and hated. She imagined her as a ghost and backed away from the wish.

I'm really happy that you are my friend, Dolly said. *I've never had a friend like you. You've made me very happy, and we have fun together.*

Jenny was confused and angry.

Why is my aunt like that? She always makes people feel bad. She wants me to die! I wish she would die!

What are you going to do? asked Dolly.

Jenny stared off into the distance. *I'm not going to do this anymore! I hate her. I can just die! Then they'll really feel bad. They'll be sorry then!*

Jenny vanished. Dolly decided to let her go.

*   *   *

Jenny found herself in a big tree on a hill looking down at the harbor.

That's what I'll do, she thought. *I don't have to pay any more attention to it; I don't even have to go back there. I'll just forget about it. Nobody can make me! I can live at the graveyard with Dolly. She loves me, and I love her, and I don't ever have to be alone again. I don't ever have to be unhappy.*

She peered at the distant ocean horizon and wished she could stop thinking.

It doesn't matter. I'm already gone. I'm already dead to everybody. It's not going to matter to anyone if I die.

She was going to find Dolly but decided against it. She didn't want to pull her friend into her unhappiness. She became overwhelmed by heavy grief. She had never felt so alone and unhappy. She needed to go find Malcolm.

*   *   *

That word you said- 'permeate'; what does it mean? Malcolm asked.

It means to surround something and fill it up. Smoke can permeate a room. When a wave washes over the beach, it permeates the sand so that after the wave goes out, your footprint fills with water when you step in the sand.

When Dolly and I were in the ant hole, we could per-

meate an ant and take it over. *When I permeate something, I envision myself as a cloud and I surround and fill that something and then I'm being it.*

Being it? Malcolm asked.

Yeah… Jenny said. *I don't know how else to describe it. If I permeate a leaf, I know what it is to be a leaf, bound to a branch while I sway in the breeze and the sunlight; I feel what it feels. In a way, I become that leaf.*

That is a good word, Malcolm said. *I've never heard that described before, but I understand what that is.* He sat for a minute, lost in thought.

You know what that actually is? he said. *That's really owning something, Jenny. That's a really good way to own something. When you permeate an ant, it's your ant; you lovingly own it for as long as you have it.*

They sat quietly for some time.

I don't know what to do, she said as Malcolm's large frame loomed over her in the darkness.

What do you want?

I want to stop hurting my mommy.

How could you do that? Malcolm asked.

I don't know! I'd have to be alive!

Could you do that?

I don't know. How could I? I have no control over that!

They sat quietly for a few moments. A police car sped by, its rotating light washing the graveyard in a momentary blue glow. Then it was gone.

What's keeping your body alive?

She looked up at him. *I-I don't… I don't know.*

What's the difference between us and people? he asked.

She looked at him, puzzled.

They have bodies, he said. *That's all.*

What?

Yeah, he said. *They have bodies. That's the only real difference.*

But they... she hesitated, trying to gather her thoughts.

They? Malcolm raised his eyebrows. *You're referring to people who are alive as they, as if you're not one of them but one of us. Dolly thinks of you as a ghost. She thinks the two of you are set forever, just playing in the clouds.*

You are a ghost. But you're a ghost that still has a body. You're caught between the two worlds, Jenny. Did you ever hear the term gave up the ghost? Do you know what it means?

No..., she replied.

It means to die, he said. *When a ghost leaves a body completely, it dies.*

Oh... Her eyes widened and she stared off. *I'm a ghost... My body is alive because I never completely left it...*

You're around it all the time, aren't you? he asked.

Yeah..., she said, as things started falling into place.

If you had left the body completely, it would have died. Are you keeping it alive?

I must be..., she mused, as a look of wonder crossed her face. *So, if I go completely back to my body, it will get well...*

Well, it's possible, he said cautiously.

The silence between them gave no indication of the torrent of thought rushing through her mind.

*   *   *

~ 7 ~

Purse Snatchers

Later that day, they were at the roof when the pigeons arrived.

I was thinking..., Dolly said.

That got Jenny's attention.

You talked about that mind that controlled the flock of pigeons. Is it a strong mind?

No, said Jenny. *Not really. It was just there.*

What if..., Dolly hesitated, *what if you were able to direct that flock of pigeons? If the mind that's directing those birds isn't strong enough...*

You think I could do that?

Dolly nodded thoughtfully.

They were ready when the flock took off from the rooftop.

Let's not be in a rush, Dolly said. *Do it gradually.*

They listened to the commands the flock was getting from its mind. They responded, as did the birds, wheeling and turning.

I'm going to do it now, Jenny said.

She realized that the first thing she had to do was *own* these birds. She decided they were her birds; she loved them, and they loved her.

The flock is swerving to the right, she decided. *There was a sudden confusion, and the flock scattered.*

65

Oops..., she said apologetically to life and the universe in general. Without interference from Jenny, the flock quickly reformed.

She gently reached out with a command and took possession of the flock again. Whatever was controlling them reeled. It reacted in confusion, threatening to again, scatter the flock, but Jenny had this. She directed the flock to fly straight in formation, then gently turn to the right. Dolly smiled as the flock complied.

Jenny cautiously guided them through simple formations, gradually getting into more sophisticated moves. After an hour, the flock was exhausted.

That's tough, she said as she landed them on the roof. *Even doing simple things you really have to focus. That mind is definitely stupid, but it does it better than I do.*

*   *   *

I want you to see something, Dolly said.

It was dark when Jenny followed her to the corner of the graveyard. The wall didn't form a corner, but curved around where the two streets met; bushes filled the triangle between the wall and the corner.

Look, Dolly said.

Jenny saw movement along the edge of the bushes. As she looked closer, she saw two teenage boys huddled in the darkness.

They're evil. They snatch purses from women who walk through here. They jump out of the bushes, grab the purse, and jump the wall to escape through the graveyard.

Wow, that's terrible, said Jenny.

We're going to stop them. Look at me.

Suddenly Dolly turned into a horrific-looking monster. It looked like a woman, but her head was cut off and floating in space above the body, gushing blood down over it.

Oh! That's terrible! Jenny said. *Why are you doing that?*

Can you create a terrible, scary image?

I guess..., Jenny said.

Let me see it; think up the most horrid monster possible, maybe the worst thing you ever saw in a horror movie.

Jenny thought for a moment. Suddenly, her face turned into that of a terrible old hag with cuts all over it that dripped blood, and she had two long fangs.

Oh, that is good! Dolly said.

Why? Jenny asked.

We're going to scare these boys like they could never imagine.

Oh! Jenny said, *we're going to perform a public service!*

Oh yes, but make sure you are visible and use your ghoul eyes.

Yes! Jenny said, laughing excitedly.

This is where they jump the wall. We'll wait here, and as soon as they grab a purse and rush toward us, we'll become visible in front of them and scream and howl. Look as terrible as you can. And if we're really good at this, we can make it so only the boys can see and hear us.

After a while, they saw a woman approaching the area where the boys waited. Jenny and Dolly watched apprehensively as she got closer.

As she passed the boys, one of them ran up behind her and snatched at her purse. But she had the strap over her shoulder, and it wouldn't release easily. The second boy came up behind her and pushed her hard, knocking her down on the grass and making her release the purse. The woman looked around and started screaming, searching for anyone to help her.

*   *   *

"Sarge, you gotta hear this."

The dark-haired female cop motioned toward two teenage boys sitting in handcuffs. They looked terror-stricken and kept glancing around as if something was after them.

"This is Jarred and Samuel. These two characters have been purse-snatching over by the graveyard. Now, you've been read your rights, and you're volunteering to answer our questions?"

"Yes," said the first boy, looking at the second, who nodded frantically.

"Yes, yes," he exclaimed.

"Jarred, tell the sergeant what you told me."

"We're not the criminals here; we were attacked."

"But," the officer interjected, "you admit to snatching the girl's purse."

"Well yeah—but..."

"Just tell him what happened."

"Well, I had grabbed the purse and she wouldn't let go, so Sammy came over and helped me."

"You mean he knocked the girl down," she clarified.

"Yeah, well… she wouldn't let go," he complained.

"And then?"

"Well, we had the purse and ran to jump over the wall and escape through the graveyard, and…"

He looked over at Sammy, who just sat wide-eyed.

"We were attacked," Jarred said.

"You were attacked," the sergeant repeated.

"Yeah…"

"By who?" the sergeant asked impatiently.

"It was by what…"

"Just tell him," the officer said.

"There were two of them," Jarred said somberly.

A look of terror came over his face as he glanced at Sammy, who looked no better.

"And?" the sergeant said.

"They were terrible. I've never seen anything like it. They were monsters… I think they were female."

"Two female monsters…" the officer said.

"Look, this was real! We really saw them! They were suddenly right in front of us!" Jarred looked across at Sammy, then at the two cops, and continued.

"Yeah! One was all bloody and her head was cut off. It floated above her body, which was waving its arms!"

"Yeah, and it was howling in our faces!" Sammy added fearfully.

"The other one was like this scary old hag. Her hair was made of long worms, and they were all wiggling."

Jarred was almost overwhelmed with fear.

"She had fangs—long fangs that went down to the bottom of her chin. And her face was oozing blood!"

"And her eyes glowed like red fire!" Sammy added.

"They knocked us down," Jarred said.

"They knocked you down?" the sergeant challenged.

"Well, I don't know. Maybe we stumbled backward," Sammy said. "I don't know it all happened so fast. It was terrible!"

"I dropped the purse," Jarred said, "and we ran down the sidewalk; that's when you guys grabbed us,".

"Well, we have you both for purse snatching. Did you do the other ones in that area?"

"Yeah..." Sammy said apologetically.

"Then that's all there is to it. You're both under arrest and will be arraigned tomorrow morning."

"Aren't you going to do something?" Jarred asked.

"Yes, we're arresting you and putting you in jail. That works for me. Doesn't that work for you?" the sergeant asked the officer.

"Yes, quite nicely," she replied.

"But what about the—we were attacked!" Jarred protested. "Those things are dangerous! Aren't you going to go after them?"

"Ah... no," the sergeant said. "Why should we?"

"Because they're dangerous!" Sammy insisted. "You should've seen them. They were..."

He stopped, shaking his head with a fearful look in his eyes.

"Only to purse snatchers," the sergeant replied.

* * *

They watched from the top of an elm tree as the boys fled the graveyard. They were a block down the street when a cop car stopped directly in front of them. Two officers jumped out with their hands on their holstered weapons and ordered the boys to stop.

The two ghosts were laughing so hard it took a while before they could speak.

That was amazing! Jenny said.

Yes.

Dolly, you come up with the best ideas ever!

Dolly just smiled and glowed.

* * *

~ 8 ~

Two Dozen Waterfalls

Jenny watched as her mother and two sisters crossed the parking lot and got into their car. As the car disappeared into the distance, she realized that Dolly was beside her.

I have a wonderful idea.

Jenny pulled her attention from the traffic and smiled at her friend. Dolly's spontaneous ideas almost always led to a wild adventure of some sort.

When I was a little girl, our family went through a rough time, and we had to stay with our cousins in New Hampshire. This place has a series of gorgeous waterfalls that stretches about two miles. The greatest joy I had as a child was playing in those falls.

Can we go there? asked Jenny.

Come, Dolly said.

A moment later, Jenny saw the falls below them as Dolly had described. The heavy winter had brought an abundance of water to New England. Its lakes and ponds were full, and its rivers ran strong, which made the falls vibrant and full.

When I was a little girl, we had so much fun playing and splashing in these falls. I haven't been back here in a long time. We have a problem, though.

Jenny looked at her quizzically.

The last time I was here, I had a body; we don't have bodies to play in the falls with... We can't just sit there and let the water run through us.

Oh..., Jenny mused. *I guess we can't.*

All the fun we have is through permeation.

Oh yes, Jenny agreed. *We borrow other bodies whether it's an ant or a bird or even a raindrop, which is a body—a body of water...*

I know what to do, Dolly said.

She went to the bank of the pool above the top falls and agitated some leaves as if they were blown by the wind.

Whoa! Jenny said. *What did you—how did you...?*

Dolly just shrugged her shoulders as the leaves drifted across the surface of the pool.

You have to teach me that! Jenny said emphatically.

Just grab a leaf! Dolly said.

As Jenny grabbed the nearest leaf, the sensation of being a ghost vanished; now she was a leaf, drifting along without a care, with Dolly beside her and treetops passing above them.

Suddenly, with a roar, they slipped over the falls. Like two tiny boats in an ocean surf, they were swept along. Tumbling and rolling, two living leaves flowed over and around rocks, tossed about at the mercy of the rapids and falls. There would be a momentary lull and then, with another roar, over they would go again swept along, tossed, and immersed. It just went on and on. It was better than any carnival ride Jenny had ever ridden—one waterfall after another in what seemed a never-ending adventure.

But eventually, they did get through the seemingly endless succession of waterfalls and arrived in a clear, natural pool where the landscape leveled out and the river widened.

Oh, this is such a beautiful place! Jenny said as they floated along, gazing at the clear blue sky above them. *Let's do it again!*

*   *   *

They were drifting in the pool at the bottom of the falls after riding them three times. Jenny released her leaf and slipped into the water. There was a huge school of tiny fish.

Just find the mind..., Dolly said softly.

Yes! said Jenny.

Jenny permeated one of the little fish; it instantly got very confused and started swimming in circles.

Wow, I've got to shut my thoughts off, she said. *These fish are super sensitive.*

Just do it like we did before, Dolly said. *Get in the school and listen; start doing what the rest of the fish do.*

Jenny fell in with the school. She could hear the thought and instantaneous response. *Go over here. Stop. React to a shadow overhead. Turn toward what might be a food source.*

This was much easier than any of the others. And for the most part, they moved lazily. *I can change that,* Jenny thought.

She started aligning her thoughts with the group mind. As she got in close to the school, her understanding of these fish heightened considerably. She spread her attention wide to take in the whole school. She had to work at it a bit, as it was a lot of fish but she got it.

As she extended herself to embrace each fish, her affection kept climbing. She felt so much love for them. They were beautiful little creatures, and if she looked carefully, she could see the sun reflecting off their scales, flashing different colors of the spectrum.

She gently intended for the school to turn to the left in a big sweeping arc. They responded beautifully. She continued to move them in more sophisticated patterns. Soon they took on the appearance of ballroom dancers, whirling and sweeping about the pool.

Oh Dolly, you have got to try this!

She gently backed off as Dolly slipped in to take control of the school. At first it was a little bumpy, but soon Dolly had them moving through all sorts of graceful gyrations.

Let's try something, Jenny said.

Dolly gave her a questioning look.

Let's split the school into two groups. You take one and I'll take the other.

Hmmm, Dolly said. *How would we do that?*

I'll send the school to the other side of the pool, then have them come right toward us. We'll both put our thoughts on the school splitting right down the middle. You take the right side and I'll take the left.

Yes, Dolly said. *That should work.*

Jenny sent them to the far end. As they started swimming toward the girls, they could see it beginning to work.

In a very natural motion, the fish simply divided.

Jenny moved in and took control of the left. She could see Dolly moving her school away from hers.

Wow, this is such fun! Dolly said. *What should we do with them?*

Let's start by moving them around in a big circle but opposite each other. This is going to be tricky, Jenny said. *I'm going to turn my school around, then take them in the opposite direction and we'll make the two schools pass through each other without any fish defecting.*

Jenny turned her school in a tight circle and started around the outer perimeter of the pool, heading toward Dolly's fish. With an effortless sweep, the two schools passed through each other. And again.

I have a good one, Dolly said. *We'll make figure eights, but when we meet in the middle, we have to cross each other's path and do it the same way, just pass through each other.*

As both schools swerved toward the middle, they looked like two halves of a polished marching band performing practiced maneuvers as they easily passed through each other.

Wow, Jenny said, *That's beautiful.*

They did it a few more times flawlessly.

The fish are getting into this, Dolly said.

Yes, we might hear, years from now, Jenny giggled, *about acrobatic fish who swim in complicated maneuvers, discovered in this pool in New Hampshire.*

Try this, Dolly said, as she suggested a rather sophisticated maneuver to the fish; they performed beautifully.

Jenny sent a pattern and then another. *The really nice thing,* she said, *is that you don't have to figure it out. You don't figure out the intricacies of it; you just get the concept of the maneuver and decide the fish are going to do it.*

The sun was going down and the pool was darkening. The ghosts thanked the fish and released them, hoping they had learned a thing or two.

I'm amazed at the way animals think, Jenny said. *They don't think like people do; they just react. They think food and go after it. They don't think about things. If a dog is thirsty, it looks for water. Dogs don't wonder where water might be, or if the water has fish in it, or about the height of the water table they just do it.*

Looking at how much thinking the average person does about unimportant subjects, she wondered if that wasn't better.

*   *   *

They hovered above the pond as dusk arrived. It was peaceful and the air felt so nice.

What's that? Jenny asked, pointing to some strange lights at the other end of the pond.

Fireflies, Dolly said.

As they glanced at each other, a thought passed between them and a moment later, they were each being a firefly.

Yes! they said concurrently.

This is even stranger than ants, Jenny thought. *Ants are so mechanical. They're so serious about their work, and they're all business. But the fireflies are gentler insects, not so serious. They seem playful, actually.*

Of all the animals they'd played with, Jenny favored the ones that flew; they were the most fun.

As she took hold of one of the flying insects, her first realization was that it was a male. The second was that only the males glowed.

Well, that's a bit unfair! Can you feel that, Dolly?

Yes, every time the light goes on, it surges. What a wonderful feeling. That's intensely pleasurable.

Why do they do that— flash on and off? Jenny asked.

Ask the bug, Dolly said.

Oh..., it tells predators that they taste really bad, Jenny said after a moment.

How?

Well, they actually do taste terrible. After a bird eats a couple of flashing bugs and realizes how awful they taste, they avoid eating flashing bugs. Simple.

Look what they're all doing, even your own bug.

Jenny looked around and discovered they were all moving toward synchronization. She could see the changing pulse of each bug moving toward alignment with the others not in exact unison, but in a musical, offset rhythm that produced an aerial dance. It was how they communicated with each other. And being in sync was important to them.

Dolly, does this light make my butt look big? she

asked, giggling.

*   *   *

~ 9 ~

The Intricacies of Endowment

The body was motionless in the bed below her. She could see the chest rising and falling slowly. *That's... mine,* she thought.

She gently reached out and touched the thick blonde hair that had continued growing during her absence. It was in beautiful condition; her mother had been brushing it daily.

It lay on its back. The casts were gone; the body was healed. She reached out and felt the scar on her skull where it had impacted the pavement.

I'm so glad they didn't have to cut the hair; that would have been terrible.

She noticed her neatly trimmed toenails with a pretty pink polish on them; again, compliments of her mother.

She wondered what would happen if she permeated the body; the thought scared her. Although she had been unconscious from her injuries when they brought her to the hospital, she had been quite conscious when the car hit her. The idea of confronting the parts of her body that had been injured made her squeamish.

I can touch the other parts, she told herself.

She reached out and touched the arm that had been uninjured. The arm had tiny, almost invisible blonde hairs on it—hairs she was sure only she had ever noticed. As she reached out and touched the palm of her hand, it moved slightly.

Wow! That reacted to me! It really is my body.

She got the odd feeling that the body was waiting for her to come along and, like the Handsome Prince, wake the sleeping beauty with just a kiss.

She remembered what Malcolm had said and decided to see if she could think happiness into the body. She thought of beautiful raindrops and rainbows after the rain. She thought of the flocks of birds she knew she could control though sometimes rather poorly. She thought of the mountain places she and Dolly had visited. She pulled this all together and directed it into the body.

She sensed a sudden lightness around the body, as if it had been tensed up for months and had finally relaxed.

Then she noticed the look of peaceful beauty on the face. It had not looked like that before. *No, it had seemed kind of dead.* She remembered how that expression always concerned her it had always looked sad.

I did that! I created happiness and gave it to the body!

She was hovering over the bed when Dolly appeared.

*   *   *

Malcolm looked up as Jenny appeared above the bench where he spent most of his time. Most ghosts had their spot; this bench was his.

You have a question, Malcolm said.

Yeah... Jenny hesitated. *You said that responsibility was owning something and causing good things for it.*

Malcolm nodded, waiting for her to continue.

But I always hear people accusing others of being responsible or not being responsible for things. It seems like a bad thing. I don't understand that.

People have been confusing responsibility with blame, Malcolm said. *Responsibility is closer to the 'permeating' that you tell me about than it is to anything else. Except maybe love. You can't really love anything unless you take responsibility for it. True responsibility is inseparable from love. I love the stories you tell me about when you permeate something—a flock of birds or an ant. That is responsibility, and it is love. How do you feel about those things you permeate?*

Oh! I feel so close to them. I feel like I really, really know them. I know what they want and how they feel.

That, said Malcolm, *is the real ownership of things. It's responsibility and love. Possession is such a crude form of ownership. Walk out on a beautiful day and own it. The reason you can control that flock is because you own it and take responsibility for it.*

*   *   *

Jenny and Dolly were hovering by the bed, listening to her mom read a story. It was about a snail who was unhappy because he could only come out of his shell when the dew was on the plants or when it was wet from rain.

It's kind of young for a 14-year-old, Jenny said, but I like listening to these stories.

Yes! Dolly agreed. *I love them. She reads stories that your little sisters will also understand and appreciate.*

Yeah, Jenny agreed.

Jenny drifted away, listening to the words that all too soon came to an end. Debbie and Lizzie had curled up together on the foot of the bed and fallen asleep. It was so peaceful.

Her mother reached out to Jenny's body and grasped her hand. Jenny moved in to envelop her mother in her sadness. She could feel how deeply her mother missed her and struggled to bear the weight of that grief. She changed position so that she could look directly into her mother's face.

If there were just some ways, I could let her know that I'm OK... that I'm still here.

Jenny was slowly being overwhelmed by her mother's sadness. She felt grief welling up inside of her. *Oh Mommy, please hear me! I'm here! And I'm OK! Please, Mommy!*

Her mother raised her chin as if she was looking right into Jenny's eyes. Suddenly, a look of shock came over her face and her eyes grew huge.

"Jenny! You're here! I can see you!"

Dolly vanished as the two younger girls suddenly awakened, startled by their mother's voice.

A nurse hurried into the room. "What's the matter? Is everything okay?"

She moved over to Jenny's body and started checking her vital signs.

"She was here! I saw her!" her mother cried.

"Who was here?" the nurse asked, startled.

"She was... my daughter. She was here. I saw her right

in front of me." She reached out her hand as if to touch the space where Jenny had been.

Jenny's world spun. She was violently pulled into her body and just as suddenly, she was slammed out, and found herself painfully huddled in the upper corner of the room.

Suddenly, alarms started going off. The nurse ran to the door and shouted for help. Another nurse, an orderly, and a doctor hurried in with a crash cart. Jenny watched as a flurry of frantic motion occurred below her. Orders were shouted. People scrambled.

Then the doctor had two paddles in his hands. He snapped a number at the orderly, who adjusted the machine.

"Clear!" the doctor shouted.

Something smashed into Jenny and everything went black.

*   *   *

One small light restrained the darkness. She huddled, wondering where she was and what had happened.

Jenny? A soft, gentle question.

Jenny became very attentive.

Jenny? It's Dolly.

Oh... she replied softly.

I thought I'd find you here.

Where am I?

At the top of an air conditioning duct. That's where you go when you want to hide.

How did I get here?

I don't know, Dolly said. *I assumed you died.*

What happened?

Well... Dolly took a breath. You appeared in front of your mother; she saw you and reacted very loudly; then suddenly alarms started going off, and there were doctors and...

Jenny suddenly remembered being in front of her mother when she started yelling and then everything had gone crazy.

My body—the alarms were going off and the doctor shocked my body with those paddles and then I...

She peered through the murky light, trying to remember.

Maybe I did die, Jenny said slowly. How would we know?

Why don't we go find out, Dolly said.

When they got to the room, she was relieved to find the body was alive, sleeping peacefully.

As they located her mother in a small waiting room at the end of the corridor, Aunt Agnes appeared beside the doctor.

"This was severe," he said. "She arrested, but we brought her back. I'm very concerned. I don't give much... I think the probability of her ever coming out of this coma is slim. And her physical condition is deteriorating. If it keeps going like this, the body will simply die or be kept alive artificially as a vegetable."

"Yes, we understand, doctor," Agnes said. "I don't think we should prolong this. I think we should remove her from all life support and just let her go. It's the right thing to do."

"No! She's there! I saw her. She was right in front of me! We can't disconnect her. She's there!" Her mother seemed to be bordering on hysteria.

"What do you mean, she was there?" Agnes asked sharply.

"I looked up, and I was looking into her eyes. I don't know how! I have no explanation. All I know is that it was my daughter!"

"Do you mean she opened her eyes?" the doctor asked.

"No, she..."

"Your daughter hasn't moved in that bed since she got here," Agnes said. "I think this has been too much for you. I'm concerned, Janice. I'm concerned for your stability. I don't think you're thinking straight. I know what it's like to lose someone like this, but we're simply prolonging the inevitable."

"No!" her mother yelled. "Neither of you understand!"

Jenny vanished.

*   *   *

The next day, her mother showed up at the regular time. Jenny cringed when she saw how haggard her mother looked. *Oh my God, she looks old!*

Two of the younger sisters were with her; they only allowed two of them to visit at a time. She sat by the bed and started talking to Jenny. Then she took out a storybook and sadly started reading.

Jenny felt Dolly's concern as her mother droned on. The sad truth was pressing down like a heavy, dark cloud: her mother was losing hope.

Dolly moved over and wrapped herself around Jenny.

She said nothing just held her.

Janice was finishing the story when Agnes barged into the room, followed by the doctor. She looked up bitterly as Agnes walked up and stood rigidly in front of her.

"I'm sorry to have to do this, but you've forced my hand." She handed Jenny's mother a folded sheet of paper. "It's a court order declaring me as her guardian. We've gotten statements from your doctor and the hospital psychiatrist."

"How..." she stuttered.

"You've been declared incompetent as her guardian. In the morning, we will do what is necessary and disconnect her from life support."

*   *   *

Dolly found Jenny tucked in a hole in the trunk of a huge tree where two massive limbs branched off. It sat on a bluff overlooking Boston Harbor. She seemed stunned, just staring blankly toward the water. Then Dolly realized she was experiencing severe grief.

After about fifteen minutes, Jenny spoke.

I did this.

She said nothing for several more minutes.

Dolly, what is it like to die? Is it going to be terrible?

Dolly answered sympathetically. *I don't remember my death. I don't know.*

Jenny continued to stare out over the water, momentarily saying nothing. *Malcolm told me to decide but I didn't. And now the decision has been taken away from me.*

Dolly wanted to hold her, but decided the best thing was just to let her be.

After a while, Dolly spoke. *I don't know what you're going to go through but I'll be with you. If you die tomorrow morning, by tomorrow evening I will have found you. And we'll find your favorite thing to do, and we'll do it. You're my sister and my best friend and nothing, not even death, can touch that. I know you'll be OK.*

She gently settled down over Jenny, surrounding and holding her with all the love she could generate.

*   *   *

~ 10 ~

The Intricacies of Connection and Disconnection

Jenny wondered why there was a small clock on the table beside her bed since she would never be able to use it, but it said 4:10 a.m. She looked down at the body below her.

I guess I am using it, she mused.

The Respirator wheezed open and shut.

How can I take any responsibility? She pleaded.

She gently settled on the blanket at her ribs. She had never really permeated this body after her accident, out of fear. She really didn't know what to expect.

Maybe little by little, she thought.

She reached out and took the right hand. It was just the hand of a 14-year-old girl, but so familiar. Her mother did her nails regularly and the nail polish was delightful. She followed the arm across her body to the left side then she withdrew.

She went to her right foot, perfectly manicured with matching nail polish to the hands. She went to the left foot and was soon able to own both of the legs.

She went to the head. She reached out and felt the blonde hair, the pale skin of the face. She then went to the stomach and the hips. From there she moved up to the chest...

Suddenly a car smashed into her, knocking her body into the air. She landed in slush, face down in a puddle. She was looking down at the body lying in the street. She couldn't breathe and her face was cold. She watched as the school bus driver knelt over the body. A wet spot appeared on his knee where it touched the pavement.

As he lifted her head out of the water, she could see her face and hair were covered with slush. Muddy water drained from her mouth and nose.

The bus driver stood aside as a paramedic took her head in her hands. Another paramedic helped her lift the body onto a stretcher. She was trembling as she watched them put the stretcher on a gurney and roll it into the back of a red ambulance.

She was fixated on the scene as the gurney was quickly rolled into the emergency entrance to the hospital. This turned into a blur of shouted orders and hands all around her, touching and probing. Then there were doctors, nurses, and orderlies moving quickly around her. Her leg was being put in a cast and then her arm. They were doing many things that Jenny didn't understand.

The gurney was rolled into her room and the body was transferred to the bed. The leg in the cast was held in the air by a cable. She looked out the window and saw the bright sun, the melted snow and the hills off in the distance.

She looked again and saw that it was dark out. It was four thirty in the morning.

That was then and this is now, she realized.

She tiredly drifted down to gently permeate the

body and finally, after all these months, slipped into a deep slumber.

*   *   *

She was startled awake. Something had hold of her, crushing her. She felt dizzy and everything was spinning. The crushing darkness was taking her away. It was a sub-zero chill, seeping into her, attempting to overwhelm.

She heard something; something very distressing, something she didn't want to hear at all. She pushed it away, but it lingered in front of her.

It was her mother crying heart-wrenching, racking sobs that would have been hard for anyone to listen to. It stung her, it ripped at her with the force of a physical rending.

The darkness pulled at her; it was pulling her away, to where she didn't know, just that it was toward the darkness.

Then there was that wretched, horrible voice that she hated.

"Doctor, how long will this take? Will she suffer? I wish to see this done promptly with minimal suffering."

That voice was melding with the darkness; it *was* the darkness. Racking pain ripped through her chest and she felt like it was being crushed.

She saw herself like mercury flowing over a surface, struggling to avoid the darkness, the pain. It pursued and engulfed her. And pulled her away from... *away from what?*

One thin filament of herself stretched back down from where she had been pulled from. It stubbornly resisted the pull and arrested the drift into the darkness.

She reached down toward where it was stubbornly anchored. As her attention reached down, there again was that heart-wrenching grief, those hacking, suffering cries.

A sharp wrenching pain snapped up that line—the grief was that of her mother.

I'm doing it again, I'm hurting my mother; I am the reason for all that pain, that grief.

She experienced a deflation of effort and realized that she was again drifting toward the darkness.

Then something snapped. It was as if she had long been encapsulated in a rock that suddenly shattered. A scream ripped itself from a depth she had never known, a scream that emanated from the full breadth of all that she was.

"Nooooo!!!"

*   *   *

As she clung with desperation to her daughter's hand, she fought the overwhelming grief that had taken hold of her. A black hand grasped her heart and squeezed as the words formed a cyclone around her.

They can't take her away from me! This can't be! I can't let her go!

Physical torture was no match for this pain. She watched them pull the breathing tube from her daughter's throat and systematically, mechanically, throw three switches in succession as a dozen lights faded and went dark.

The body jerked in the bed in a sick dance, a sinful mockery of the life that dangled in the dying body, all tailored toward her suffering.

"I'm sorry, it'll all be over in a moment." The doctor's voice seemed far away.

The hand she held between her hands seemed cold, so cold it scared her. Then the body jerked again and slumped as a sharp terror grabbed her.

She was watching the most horrible thing she could ever imagine the cruel, painful thrashing of her daughter's death throes. She was in hell, being forced to watch this; she didn't want to look, she didn't want to see this but she couldn't look away.

The body jerked again as it suddenly sat straight up. Then with a huge gasping inhale of breath, her eyes popped open.

As her mother stared into those eyes, they blazed with recognition.

The End

Epilogue

Home at Last

Jenny's atrophied muscles confined Jenny to a wheelchair on the front porch, her mother sitting beside her in a rocking chair.

Physical therapy would be needed to get Jenny back on her feet, and a tutor would be hired to help her catch up on the education she'd missed in the spring.

"I listened to your stories, every day. I heard what you said to me."

"Somehow... I knew that," her mother said slowly. "I don't know how, but I knew."

They stared out toward the intersection where it all began and to the graveyard beyond.

"I wasn't alone," Jenny said.

Her mother looked startled, then bewildered.

"What?"

"I had someone with me; there was someone there the whole time I was in the coma."

"I don't understand," her mother said. "That's... a little scary."

"There's a lot that's hard to understand," Jenny replied. "Do you remember, about a week ago, when you were reading to me and you looked up and saw a vision of me standing in front of you?"

"Yes! I saw you!"

"I was there, *trying so hard* to let you know I was still here... and that I was okay."

"I knew that I, I knew..." Her mother was struggling with disbelief.

"There was someone with me," Jenny said softly. "Someone who loves me very much. When I came back..." her voice broke, "I left her behind..., but I had to come back... I—"

Jenny's eyes filled with tears as a single drop traced its way slowly down her cheek.

"How but how could that be?" her mother whispered.

Jenny only shrugged and looked across at the graveyard.

There was silence for a few moments.

"I miss her so badly..." she whispered. Her voice trembled, and she struggled to contain the grief.

They sat in silence, both gazing toward the intersection.

Jenny wondered if Dolly was at the graveyard; her mother simply wondered.

After a while, her mother turned to Jenny, her eyes soft and full of care.

"After everything we've been through... it would be foolish not to believe you. I'm ready to listen. Tell me the whole story."

Jenny's shoulders relaxed as she let out a breath. She looked across at the graveyard, gathering herself.

"She was with me the whole time... Her name is Dolly."

*   *   *

Ghosts
Are People, Too

Trilogy of the Ghosts

Book Two

By

Christopher Mercon

Prologue

The storm that had thundered through the night ended in the early morning, leaving a dark ceiling of clouds that soon turned to gold. The air had an ozone-fresh smell, and the morning felt newly washed. The crisp colors of the trees glowed in the slanted rays of sunlight.

Her mother had a handyman build a small ramp at the front door so she could wheel her chair onto the porch. This became her favorite place where she was sheltered from rain as well as the harsh midday sun.

She noticed a snail crawling across a broad leaf on one of the bushes that lined the porch railing. Its slow, deliberate movement was mesmerizing.

She could feel the coiled structure of the shell arching above her and the rough texture of the leaf beneath her. She had become the snail. Her skin was pleasantly moist, but she felt a flicker of concern as the sunlight warmed her shell. If her skin began to dry, she would have to retreat into her shell and seal it tight waiting until the cool dew of night made it safe again.

Fifteen minutes later, having soaked up all the warmth she could handle, she slowly withdrew into her shell, leaving behind a slimy coating to ensure it would seal properly against the leaf and prevent moisture loss.

It was dark and damp. As the sun heated the shell, she slipped into a deep, contented sleep.

Yes! I've still got it!

She found herself back in her wheelchair. This was the first time she had successfully achieved permeation since awakening from the coma. Doubts had crept in since her recovery. She had assumed her abilities were gone, left behind when she ceased being a ghost.

But this... this was a relief. *I can still do it.*

Still, she hadn't yet been able to leave her body like she used to; not fully. Not the way she could before waking from the coma.

~ 1 ~

Recuperation

Jenny started awake.

Something, someone is here...

She remained still and listened. She extended her aware-ness, trying to perceive anything any motion, any noise.

"Oh my god!" she whispered; tears flooded her eyes.

Her mother, Janice, entered the bedroom. "Honey, what is the matter?"

Jenny stared blankly into space.

"What is it?" her mother urged.

When Jenny turned her head distractedly, she got concerned.

"Would you tell me what is going on? Please?"

"It's Dolly"

"What?" her mother asked.

Jenny said nothing but scanned the room and the space beyond.

"That—ghost?"

Jenny's chin dropped into what Janice real-ized was a nod.

"What? What is happening with Dolly?"

"She's back..."

"What? Jenny, wake up! You're having a nightmare!"

"She's here..."

"Where?" her mother asked.

"She's here! I can't..."

"I think you're just having a nightmare."

The look that came into Jenny's eyes startled her mother.

"If she's really here, why can't you see her? Where is she?"

Janice studied her daughter, saying nothing.

"She's here! I know her; I know when she's around!"

Janice gave a frustrated sigh. *I don't know how to handle this; it is definitely not in the parenting manuals.*

"This is terrible!" Jenny said. "Do you believe me?".

"I believe in you. If you say that this is what is happening, then my job is to get you through whatever you're going through. It's going to be fine," she said as she studied her daughter thoughtfully. "But if she is here, why can't you see her?"

"I don't know..."

After a moment of silence, Janice spoke. "OK..., you told me about the last time you saw Dolly just before you came out of the coma; do you remember?"

"What?" asked Jenny.

"What she said to you."

"What?" Jenny demanded.

"If you die tomorrow, I will find you. You're my sister, and my best friend and nothing, not even death, can touch that."

"Wow...," Jenny said as she looked up at her mother, "you remember that?"

"Yeah, it made a bit of an impression on me."

Jenny said nothing as she sat, upright in her bed, gazing straight ahead.

"So, what are you worrying about, then?" her mother said, challenging her.

"What do you mean?" Jenny asked, looking bewildered.

"You don't believe her? You don't think what she said was true?"

Jenny's chin slowly dropped as she thought back.

"That's right," Jenny said as her eyes got bigger and the tears vanished. "I had forgotten..."

"I think..." her mother said, "I don't know... maybe she's trying to find you. Maybe she's looking..., or..."

"Yes! Thank you, mommy!" she said as she reached to her mother to her in a grateful hug.

*　　*　　*

Jenny looked at the street below; so familiar, yet different in the light of the full moon. The darkened green leaves in the tree in the front yard looked remarkable; the leaves surrounding the streetlights seemed to emit their own illumination.

Jenny was awakened with a sudden jerk. Her whole body was caught in an uncomfortable tension; she hated waking this way. She turned over and somehow, managed to get back to sleep.

*　　*　　*

Autumn was arriving late and the nights were still warm. The perfect wind carried her through the surrounding trees as her gaze caught the moon's reflection off the surface of the pond on the next block. The graveyard was a dark patch that interrupted the grid of lights across the land.

Boston glowed in the distance with lights that reminisced her time as a ghost. Her thoughts drifted back to when she and dolly would linger over the city or the graveyard or the times they would watch the sun set and the moon climb across the sky. Back when she was... *maybe...*

She gazed down at her house and the graveyard in the distance.

I'm out! My body is in my bedroom asleep but I'm outside, above the trees!

Suddenly, something encompassed her, filled her; something so familiar...

DOLLY!!!

She seemed to be everywhere as her smiling face illuminated. The ghost surrounded her, embracing her, frolicking like a puppy. Then she was experiencing pure pleasure that lifted her into ecstasy as Dolly permeated her.

You're back! Jenny cried. *I knew you would come back! Even my mother knew you would!*

Dolly got a look of surprise.

She knows?

She knows all about us! She's your mother too! Remember?

Oh, my gosh, Jenny. I never thought...

How could I not tell her? How could I keep you secret? You're one of the most important things in my life. I couldn't keep the two people that I love the most, ignorant of each other.

And she's fine with it?

Yes! She's the one that insisted that we would find each other!

Wow! Dolly beamed.

*   *   *

"Mom! Dolly's back! This is so good. I am so happy to be with her again."

"Wow, you certainly look happier," her mother said cautiously.

Jenny was suddenly worried. "I assumed you believed me. I even told Dolly…"

The joy drained from Jenny's face, replaced by serious concern.

"I think I made a big mistake," Jenny said. "I shouldn't be talking about this."

As she glanced up, their eyes locked.

"Look, I'm your mother; I want you to be able to discuss anything with me. "

Jenny gave a frustrated sigh and stared off.

"Talk to me," her mother said.

"I don't know if you believe me. Sometimes it seems so crazy that *I* have a hard time believing it myself."

"Then just tell me about it."

"She's just another girl; she's my best friend! I don't know what else to tell you…"

Her mother gazed into her eyes, hoping she would continue.

"It's not…" Jenny started to say something but then

stopped. "It's not like Voodoo or magic. I know a lot of ghosts and most of them are really nice people. Can I call them people?" she wondered aloud. "They call us people. But they're just people without bodies, that's all. Once they had bodies and had babies and jobs and families and houses. And then their bodies died and they became ghosts. And that's all they are—people without bodies."

"What about the afterlife and heaven and hell?" her mother asked.

As Jenny shrugged her shoulders, she recalled Dolly doing the same.

"I don't know; they don't know. Most of them seem to believe in God. My ghost friend Malcolm is a Christian and goes to church every Sunday. A lot of ghosts go to church."

We don't go to church, Dolly thought as she eavesdropped on the conversation between Jenny and her mother. She was surprised that Jenny was unaware of her presence.

"This is a struggle for me," Janice said.

"Why?"

"How could it be otherwise?" Her mother stared off for a moment before she continued.

"We had a seemingly normal existence until one day you are hit by a car and end up in the hospital in a coma. After months of hoping, after having my custody and control of you snatched away by my sister who wanted to terminate you by taking you off life support, you suddenly, at the most horrific moment of my life, return to me in a miracle. I was going to have my daughter back and my life was going to return to normal."

"Yeah..." Jenny said guardedly.

"Then I discover that there is nothing normal about *any of this*; I find out that while you were in a coma, you were off having fun with an actual ghost who has a grave, a name and a past! And then I have to reconcile myself to a completely new reality where my beautiful 14-year-old daughter is actually some sort of a medium whose best friends are ghosts!"

Jenny looked a bit stunned.

"I'm not saying I don't believe you," her mother said, "I do believe you; it's just difficult. I've had to adjust my thinking in a lot of ways to even *begin* to accept any part of this."

"Do you think it was easy for me?" Jenny asked. "I cannot recall a time when I had a normal existence. Imagine what it's like as a little girl who could not go out at night without seeing an apparition peering down at her from the branches of a tree or from behind a bush. I felt like such a freak and I was afraid to tell anyone about it. If I didn't' have people like Dolly or Malcolm to guide me through it, I would have lost my mind. When I was going through my biggest challenge, Dolly was there to get me through it. When I figured out that Aunt Agnes was trying to kill me, it was Malcolm's advice and guidance that got me to find my way back to you."

"I didn't realize..." her mother muttered.

* * *

Janice was standing just inside the bathroom hovering over Jenny who had her wheelchair parked against the tub that was filled with hot water. She had untied the front strap and slipped her bathrobe off her shoulders; she was struggling to get out of the wheelchair and into the tub.

"I wish you would let me help you."

"Not a chance," her daughter said.

As Jenny carefully, successfully lowered herself into the hot water, she groaned.

"Oh yes, I needed this! I'm going to be here a while. I'll be fine, I won't drown; you can go do whatever you need to do."

Before her mother got a chance to respond, she suddenly turned, listening off. "That's the doorbell I wonder who..." Her words trailed off as she left.

When Janice got to the front door, she looked through the sidelight but couldn't see whoever was there. She pulled the door open to see a pretty, brown-haired girl about Jenny's age. She had on an expensive pink sweatshirt and designer jeans.

"Hello!" she said, smiling. "What can I do for you?"

Is Jenny available? I heard she was home from the hospital and I wondered...

Jenny didn't have many close friends. *This is a good thing!* Janice thought. *She'll need more friends when she starts back to school.*

"She's in the bathtub. Can you wait?"

Oh yes! I'm very eager to see her. Can you tell her I'm here?

"Come in, please." She swung the door open and invited the girl into the foyer. "Get comfortable; who should I say is here?" her mother said as she turned and started toward the bathroom.

Just tell her it's Dolly.

Her mother froze. *This is some sort of practical joke!*

"Who did you say?"

Dolly. I'm sure she's mentioned me. We're best friends.

Her mother slowly turned and stared. Everything stopped as she tried to grasp the situation. *It can't be... but why would a girl come to our front door and say this?*

"Who are you?" Janice demanded angrily.

I'm...Dolly.

"What? She thinks you're a—No! You can't be! You're..."

I know..., the girl said as she shrugged her shoulders. *I am Dolly.*

Jenny had been soaking in the tub for about forty minutes. About ten minutes ago the water had cooled sufficiently that she had to add hot water and it was again cooling. She wondered where her mother was and who was at the door. It must be someone important as it was out of character for her not to have checked on Jenny every fifteen minutes.

She pulled the plug and lowered herself as the water receded, to avoid the intrusion of the cool air on her wet skin. When the tub was empty, she pulled the towel from the towel rack above her and dried thoroughly. She again wondered what her mother was doing as she pulled herself back into the wheelchair and slipped into her bathrobe.

As she entered the living room, she was surprised to see Dolly sitting on the couch chatting with her mother. It was a bit more than a surprise; it was surreal.

*　　*　　*

~ 2 ~

Chatan

When Dolly appeared beside her on the front porch, Jenny slipped a bookmark into the page and closed the book she had been reading.

You've been with Mom, Jenny said.

Dolly smiled with a shyness that Jenny rarely saw in her. *When I saw her go to the gazebo with a cup of coffee and a newspaper, I couldn't stay away.*

I'll bet she didn't get to read her newspaper, Jenny said, laughing.

No. We've been spending quite a bit of time getting to know each other. Is that, OK?

Of course! Jenny insisted. *I am so glad. Everything is working out so well! And I've taken to teasing my mother about how I am not the only one who has a friend who is a ghost.*

It's an ongoing interview, Dolly said.

Really? About what?

Everything! She has so many questions especially about history.

*   *   *

A man appeared on the sidewalk, looking up at Jenny. He was tall, dark-haired, and handsome, with high cheekbones.

"You must be Jenny," he said, smiling.

"Yes! Who are you?"

"My name is Chatan. Your mother hired me to get you on your feet and back into school."

"Are you my tutor or physical therapist?"

"Both, it would seem."

"How do you come to be both?" Jenny asked.

"Well, I am a professional tutor. Most of my clients are children many of whom miss school because of injuries and need both services. So, I went to school and got certified as a physical therapist. It's very efficient, and I've become quite sought after."

"Good," Jenny said. "When can we start?"

"Today, if you wish."

"I do!"

"What is your name, miss?" he asked, turning toward Dolly.

Both girls stared in surprise. After a moment, Dolly spoke.

You can see me?

"Quite well," he said.

How? Dolly asked.

"Do you know what she is?" asked Jenny.

He nodded toward Jenny as he responded to Dolly. "I see your world and hers as one, indivisible. Where her world stops, yours starts; one flows into the other seamlessly."

"But you are quite embedded in her world," he said, turning to Jenny. "Am I correct?"

"Oh, yes," Jenny said. "As she is in mine."

"Mr. Farplain, thank you for coming. I see you've met Jenny."

Jenny turned to see her mother standing in the doorway.

"Yes," he replied. "And her friend as well."

She stopped and stared. "How can you see her? I've only recently..."

"I've been in touch with spirits all my life. It's part of my culture."

"What culture?" Jenny asked.

Cherokee, said Dolly.

Chatan was stunned. "Yes, that's amazing! How did you know?"

I was one of the spirits that your people were in touch with, but it was quite a long time ago maybe two hundred years. It was when I was wandering in the southern Appalachian Mountains—Tennessee and the Carolinas.

"Wow. I would love to hear more about them, maybe later. That is a remarkable dress you wear," he said. "Did your mother make it?"

I made it. It was under her tutelage, but I sewed every stitch, a long, long time ago.

"Nice work," he said. "If that dress existed today, in that condition, it would be worth several thousand dollars."

"Well, this is a remarkable start," Janice said.

"Please, come in."

*   *   *

Janice converted one of the rooms on the ground floor into a combination classroom and clinic. It had double French doors that opened onto the porch that covered three sides of the house, making that an extended class-room as well as clinic on warm afternoons. She was sitting on the porch with Chatan, Jenny, and Dolly.

"How do you want to do this?" Janice asked Chatan.

"It works best if we study in the morning, right after breakfast, and work on physical therapy in the afternoon."

"Oh?" asked Janice.

"Yes," Chatan said. "I will push her fairly hard in the physical therapy; she'll be too exhausted to study."

"Oh yes, that sounds good," Janice said.

*   *   *

"I want to know all about your culture," Jenny said, "especially the part where you can see ghosts."

"When I was young, probably five years old, I had a ghost friend. She was an older woman. I thought she was my guardian angel, and maybe in a way, she was."

"She was Cherokee," he continued, "and very insistent that I learn the traditional ways of my ancestors. She was concerned that they would be lost forever. She taught me many things, most of them spiritual, about my people; things that had been lost over time. She told me that I had been chosen to be the guardian of the knowledge and tra-ditions of our people. Later, I found out that she was my great-great-grandmother."

"What do you do with that knowledge?" Janice asked.

"I wrote a book and got it published; it did better than I expected. But more importantly, the story of the Cherokee beliefs and traditions is now a matter of record. I've been recognized as the leading authority on the subject. Now, it will never be lost."

"That's wonderful!" said Janice.

"I thought I was the only child who talked to ghosts," Jenny said.

"A lot of children have the ability to see ghosts, and to communicate with them," he said. "The culture has come to refer to them as a child's 'imaginary friend,' but they're real."

*   *   *

"I would tutor you both," Chatan said.

Yes! Dolly said.

"Why?" Jenny asked.

"I feel she has a lot to offer," he said. "I can have the two of you work together on some projects, and it would make it fun. She's not doing anything but hanging around listening; she should participate."

"Yeah," Jenny said. "That will be fun."

"I don't think I can teach you anything about history," Chatan said to Dolly. "Your knowledge is far greater than mine. Study as you would. I'm simply going to have Jenny study the various chapters as we go along. Then she will have an extended open discussion about the lesson with you and me. Then Jenny will write a paper on the chapter."

"I would like that," Jenny said.

"But physics is another story. Your knowledge is fairly good on the subject, but I imagine Dolly will need a bit of work. We may do something similar. We'll see."

"Plus," he added, "I've never tutored a ghost. That would really rock my resume!"

Jenny shook her head and giggled.

Before they could continue, the door opened and Janice entered.

"I have lunch ready."

"I can smell the coffee," Chatan said.

"Bring your sister," Janice said to Jenny.

*   *   *

A week later, Jenny was able to stand and was beginning to slowly walk.

"She will be walking quite well in a week," Janice said.

"She'll be running in a month," Chatan answered.

"Your healing abilities are quite something," Janice said.

"I do not heal her," Chatan said. "She alone can"

"What?" Jenny demanded. "What are you talking about? The healing is happening right in front of our eyes."

"Yes," he said. "Your healing is wonderful, but it is not my accomplishment it is yours. Aside from establishing a regimen, I merely direct the healing, channel, and encourage it; only the spirit can heal the body."

*　　*　　*

It was a windy, sunny day. The clouds above the grave-yard cascaded high above the city, producing a glorious effect as they raced across the sky. Jenny was walking to the store to get some things for her mother.

Hey! This is wonderful! Dolly said from high above her. *It's such a beautiful day!*

Suddenly, Jenny was with Dolly, above the trees, watching the agitation of the branches as they were tossed back and forth by the wind. The land stretched off in all directions below them.

Where are you going? Dolly asked.

To the store to get... Jenny cried out. "Ahh! Ow!"

Jenny was sitting on the sidewalk, obviously in pain.

What happened? asked Dolly.

Darn! I walked into the stupid pole!

Well, you can't do that! Dolly scolded.

Do what? Jenny asked irritably.

You can't leave your body walking down the street while you're off in the clouds. It's no different than a car rolling down the street with no one driving it.

Jenny struggled to her feet, knowing that Dolly was right.

That scares me a little, Dolly said. *You could have walked out into traffic. I assumed you knew how to do this and stay out of trouble.*

Wow... Yeah, I guess you're right. I hadn't

thought of that.

They continued down the street, Dolly walking beside Jenny.

I hope I don't have a black eye, Jenny mumbled. It was a lesson she would remember.

* * *

~ 3 ~

The Thaddeus P. Thayer Middle School

It was an old school; a historical landmark. It was built with a lot of wood and extensive ornamental design woodwork throughout. It seemed archaic but Jenny liked that.

As they started up the wide concrete stairs to the front door, Dolly said goodbye and disappeared.

She had been through this routine in the past but this time she had received, in the mail, a computer printout of everything she needed to know—her homeroom number, her locker number as well as the combination, among other things. She was settled in by lunch. That first day turned into the first week, and her routine was established and she was comfortable with it.

*   *   *

It was a Tuesday night and she was alone in her room doing her homework. The day before she had worked on a history assignment but hadn't finished it. It was due tomorrow, but she couldn't find it. She had put a lot of work into the piece, and the fact that it was lost worried her.

I wonder if I left it in my locker! Oh, that would not be good...

She again searched for it; she looked through her knapsack and all her other papers and then searched her room.

Yeah, it must be there.

She sat at her desk trying to find a solution.

Oh! I can go check...

She suddenly found herself in the darkened corridors of her school. The ancient woodworking made it look spooky in spite of the well-lit 'exit' signs at the end of each corridor. She found her locker easily enough. She even found the report she was working on.

What good does it do me sitting there? I can't do anything with it.

Young lady, what are you doing here at this time? Students cannot be in the school after it is closed!

Startled, she turned to see a man about sixty years of age with a handlebar mustache and a string tie. He reminded her of Mark Twain. And he was a ghost.

She felt it best to simply answer his question.

I left my history assignment in my locker and I need to finish it tonight.

How do you come to be here? he asked.

Necessity, mostly, she replied.

Young lady, I don't think it's advisable to be flippant. I think you fully understood my question and chose to respond in a manner that is unbecoming of a young lady in pursuit of an education.

I'm sorry, she responded. *It's just a difficult question to answer.*

I understand, he said. *I'll rephrase it. How are you able to be here? You're not a ghost. I've seen you in school. Unless of course, you perished in the last several hours, which I doubt would be the case.*

I spent a lot of time in a coma and I learned from necessity, she replied. *My friend Dolly is a ghost; a lot of my friends are ghosts.*

You are a medium? he asked. *If you are, you seem to have extraordinary talent.*

I never thought about that, but I guess I am. My friend Malcolm, another ghost, says that I'm stuck between two worlds, but that seems a bit overly dramatic to me.

It would seem to me that you are stuck in neither, as you seem to operate in both.

I guess so. I don't give it much thought. I'm a person with a body, and I can leave that body and operate like a ghost.

What is your name? he asked.

Jenny. What is yours?

Thaddeus.

Is that your name on the front of the school?

It would seem, he said, nodding his head slightly. *What are you going to do about your assignment?*

I don't have an answer to that. I didn't think it through.

It's a malady of the young, he said. *How soon could you be here in your corporeal form?*

My what?

The word is corporeal, Mistress Jenny. It means 'of the body.' It's from the Latin 'Corpus.' The word corpse also comes from that term. If you don't understand the meanings of words and their origin, you can't be educated.

She thought for a moment. *Oh, when can I come*

here in my body?

Yes, your corporeal form.

About fifteen minutes.

You are aware of the rear exit to the playground?

Yes, she replied.

Come in through there, he said as he vanished.

*   *   *

Jenny rose from her bed. Dolly was smiling at her.

I perceive an adventure, she said.

Yes, I left my history assignment at the school and I have to go get it.

How do you get into the school? It's closed.

Someone's going to let me in.

Wow, Dolly said. Let's go!

She headed down the stairs. As she grabbed her jacket off the hook in the hallway, her mother busted her.

"Young lady, where are you going at this time of night?"

That's the second time in an hour I've gotten busted. I need to stop being so careless.

"I need to get my history assignment from my locker at school. I forgot it and I've got to get it done tonight."

"At this time of night? How can you even get into the school?"

"Well, someone is going to let me in."

"Who? Who would be there this late?"

"Well, he's a ghost..." she said cautiously.

"What? Oh, of course," she said, shaking her head.

"I'm just going to hurry over there, get it and hurry

back. It'll be fine."

"It's not safe, you going out after dark. You re-member Jeremy?"

Ouch! I never thought she'd play that card.

"I'll have Dolly with me."

"What can she do?"

"Do you remember the story about the muggers near the graveyard, the ones that were stealing purses?"

"Yes."

"Dolly can be the scariest creature you've ever seen. Believe me."

Her mother hesitated. "How long will it take you to get there and back?"

Jenny knew she had won. "Maybe an hour."

"Dolly?"

Yes, ma'am, she said as she appeared beside Jenny.

"You're going with her?"

Yes, ma'am, she replied.

"OK, you two stay together! Dolly, I don't want her out of your sight for a moment."

Yes, mommy, she replied, smiling.

"Oh, just go, the both of you," she said sup-pressing a smile.

Two teenage girls, my goodness.

Forty minutes later Jenny was in her room, finishing her history assignment.

*   *   *

Later, while the body slept, Jenny returned to the school.

Thank you, sir, Jenny said.

Thaddeus looked down at her.

Yes. Well, we can't have you failing to complete an assignment.

Jenny had a knack for finding mentors. Chatan had become a good friend who she could go to for advice and guidance even after he had completed his work with her. At the graveyard, it was Malcolm; at her school, it was the gruff old educator, Thaddeus. Lately Jenny found she was spending a lot of time with him. She loved history and was impressed by his knowledge and understanding. He cultivated her interest and was eager to help with her studies.

One night she was studying World War I but had many questions; she went to see Thaddeus.

It's all lies, he muttered.

What? she asked, wide-eyed.

Yes, history books are so many lies! Yes, the Allied powers won and the stories of the valiant victories were true. But how and why the war happened? It's all rubbish. There is no such thing as a just war. There are just responses but before that point, there were a lot of occurrences that were designed to bring about conflict.

Jenny was a bit shocked to hear this. She considered her textbooks to be inviolate, almost sacred.

History books are written by the victors, often by the perpetrators. War is the most profitable endeavor that mankind has ever engaged in. Anything that is used to produce a profit whether it is war, crime, disease, or poverty—anything that is used to produce profit will proliferate.

Proliferate? she asked.

Yes, the word means to expand, to grow and become plentiful. If honesty and integrity were profitable, we would have an abundance of such. But alas, they are not.

The world, he continued, *will always be ruled by a few. If those few do not possess honesty and integrity, then the society will suffer. The original leaders who established this Democratic Republic were, for the most part, honest, good men with integrity. I knew some of them. But one day, they are gone and those with a profit motive, with a political agenda that they consider supreme, they will rule.*

*　　*　　*

~ 4 ~

Dark Concepts and Angry Emotion

As Jenny left the cafeteria and headed to her English class, she spotted someone she knew from elementary school.

"Jason!" she said as she approached him. "Hi, it's Jenny! Don't you remember me?"

He glanced down with a serious look on his face.

"Yeah, how're you doing?" he mumbled.

"I'm good. How have you been?"

"Well, OK, I get by."

He seemed unfriendly and didn't want to talk. He was standing with a sour-looking kid with a scowl on his face. She sensed a good bit of hostility from him.

"Well, it was good to see you again," Jenny said as she edged away, turned, and headed down the corridor.

Dolly appeared beside her. *What was that about?*

I used to live next door to him and we were best friends from the time we were toddlers and through elementary school. When I was in the fifth grade, his family moved away and I haven't seen him since. But this is a different person. There's a real darkness about him, something that makes me uncomfortable. And the boy he is with is just plain evil. I wonder what happened to Jason.

That's his name? Dolly asked. *Jason?*

Yeah, she replied sadly.

They're both extremely dark, Dolly agreed.

*   *   *

Later that night Jenny mentioned him to Thaddeus.

Yes, he said grimly. *That boy will be trouble, mark my words.*

You know who it is that I'm talking about?

Yes, he stands out, the educator said. *He and that other youngster that he is friends with. His name is Robert; his colloquial name is Bobby.*

Colloquial? Jenny asked.

The word means informal. It is common speech, used by those who are not highly educated. They don't understand the meanings of words and so they degrade speech.

You often speak of how important the meanings of words are, Jenny said. *I've been studying the definitions of words that I encounter.*

Pay attention to the etymology of the words, he advised.

Etymology? she wondered aloud.

It is the study of the origin and development of words, he replied. *The definitions and usage of a word change and evolve through time. Studying the etymology of a word brings about a greater understanding of a language and the history of the people who spoke it. People think in words. They communicate with words. If they don't know the meaning of words, they can neither think properly nor communicate properly.*

"People think in words..." Jenny whispered aloud.

Tree, he said. *What happens when I say that?*

I see a tree, she said. *A large leafy tree with a thick trunk.*

Yes. When I say a word, you get a thought from that. Am I correct?

Y-yes, she said thoughtfully.

Ocean, building, automobile. Words inspire thought.

Yes, I see that, she said.

And when I say many people collect the aesthetic external skeletons of gastropods?

She looked confused. *I, uh, I don't know.*

How is your thinking at this moment? he asked.

Confused...

Yes, because if you don't have a meaning for a word, you can't think with it. Aesthetic means possessing beauty; a gastropod is the animal that lives in a seashell. The shell is its skeleton; external means he wears it on the outside. How is your thinking now?

Good, she replied. *They collect sea shells.*

How can people think properly if they don't know what a word means? Or if they think that recuperate means regurgitate? I think a thought. Do you know what it is?

No... she said.

Of course not. I need to express that thought in words. I speak and you hear the words; if you understand those words, then you have that thought. And we are able to communicate.

I never knew words were that important, she said.

More important than any other education; you can't

solve mathematical problems if you don't understand the mathematical terms. I daresay, you would be stupid in mathematics or at best, not as accomplished in the subject as you would be, were you fully educated in the terms of that subject. If you were to ask a number of students, how many would even know the definition of the word 'mathematics' or even 'arithmetic,' or the difference between the two? And yet they study a subject which they cannot define.

Stupid? she asked.

All stupidity comes from not understanding the meanings of words. All stupidity.

I don't want to be stupid, she said, sounding genuinely concerned.

Learn the meanings of words! There are a beauty and aesthetic to words that most people today never come to know. It is a joy when you get a thought and are able to express it properly in words that convey your concept well.

It is the first thing a child learns, he continued. *From very early in his life a child is learning to recognize the words that his parents are saying to him. His success in life is largely determined by how well he learns to understand those words.*

*　　*　　*

Jenny was distracted from her homework as her thoughts drifted back to her encounters with Thaddeus the night before. She put his name in a search engine and was surprised at what she found. Born in 1750, he was a well-known educator and author, as well as an adviser to three presidents. He was the headmaster of her school from the time it was built in 1811 until his death in 1831. Her school was an historical landmark that was given his name after he passed.

He's here because it's his school... My school is 200 years old! Or rather, his school. But that's not that unusual in New England.

When her homework was finished, she lay on her bed, thinking of the many things Thaddeus was teaching her. She realized that when you really learn history, the present looks quite different. She had never met anyone who had such a love for history and for learning. He seemed to come alive when he was teaching her, especially when he was going over the subtleties of some critical event in history. His excitement and interest were infectious.

*　　*　　*

What is that? Dolly asked.

They were above the street that passed by her school. It was late summer, and the nights were starting to feel like autumn.

Jenny didn't respond but continued to stare off into the distance. Dolly could make out two boys casually walking along the next block.

It's Jason and Bobby, Jenny said.

One of the boys stopped to light a cigarette and then caught up with the other.

Is that the boy you knew when you were a little girl?

Yeah, Jenny said as she moved closer to the boys. She followed their progress as they went behind the school. As they sat on a bench inside the playground, one of them pulled out a bottle. From its size and shape, she could tell that it was some sort of liquor probably whiskey. Listening to their slurred speech, she realized they were already quite drunk. Every fifth word was a cuss word. It struck her how different he was from the boy she knew in her childhood. She thought back to the days in elementary school and even earlier.

I remember the two of us being in the same playpen! Oh my gosh. I had forgotten that.

Dolly said nothing but listened as she continued.

He was my best friend for years. We did everything together. Our mothers used to take turns switching off babysitting. We slept in the same crib. Oh my gosh! We took baths together!

The two boys were sitting quietly, probably in a drunken stupor. She settled over Jason. As she permeated him, she felt a disorientation and dizziness and realized that it was the liquor. His space was thick with... she couldn't quite find the words. She perceived the bitterness and the hate. Then she perceived the terror.

Why is Jason in such terror? Where did that come from?

She reeled as she encountered dark, evil images—dreams of unspeakable things. All of this hatred and fear and evil were held in a soup or a glue. At the center of this she found his self, what she recognized as his ghost. Her self, the ghost, was free to come and go. She could roam the skies or become the butterfly, a bird, or even a flower.

But with Jason—his self, his soul, was encapsulated at the core of this emulsion of hate, fear, and loathing. It was so strong; it was like a foul chemical fire that burned red hot. But there was something that bound it all, like a sticky cloud. It almost felt like thick, fibrous, mental vomit.

She realized that she was still looking for that little boy that shared her crib at the age of two. She extended herself to that dark center, but what she reached was his terror. Her world was suddenly collapsing. This happened in the space of a few seconds.

She tried to retreat into herself, to desperately hide, to avoid—*how can fear be that bad, that powerful?* She trembled as a volcano of gut-wrenching emotional lava washed over her. *I don't want to live; I don't want to go on like this. I am no good! I am EVIL. I don't deserve to live.* She welcomed the darkness as she plunged deeper...

Then something, someone had her. She was forcefully pulled—she cried out as she woke in her bed, shaking and almost hysterical with grief and fear.

Dolly was all around her like a warm gentle wind or the most soothing, beautiful music she had ever heard. She clung to her as the darkness slowly lifted. She felt so dirty, as if she needed to go run a shower, much too hot, and just scrub her skin until she was raw and red.

Hey sweetheart, how are you doing? Her voice was so gentle, so sweet. Tears poured from Jenny's eyes as the cold evil seemed to evaporate.

Come with me, Dolly said as she lifted at Jenny.

Jenny shook her head, afraid to move.

Come. Dolly's voice was soothing.

Slowly, Jenny was lifted away from the body as Dolly led her to the roof. They hovered in front of the huge tree that filled the corner of the backyard.

Look around.

Jenny looked at the broad trunk.

I want you to look at where you are. That's your house. This is your yard, and that is your street. You're not in Jason you're here. Come.

Then they were in her youngest sister's bedroom. Two little heads made quite a pile of blonde hair on the pillow. Jenny smiled.

Debbie and Lizzie, she said. *They're twins; they won't* sleep *without each other. They are so adorable.*

Dolly smiled. *Let's go see the other two.*

Dawn seemed the epitome of innocence and naivete with her blond hair spread across the pillow.

And the other? Dolly asked.

Wendy, the fearless, Jenny said, *the athlete, the achiever.*

She's a brunette, Dolly whispered.

Yes, like me. The other three are blonde.

Come, Dolly said.

They were back in her room looking down at her sleeping form.

Wow, Jenny sighed. I never really just stop and look at it. She is so pretty...

What is this? Dolly asked, pointing at a trophy.

Oh, I won that in Cross Country in September, before the accident; 1st place.

What is this?

Oh, that's a conch. I found that while visiting some friends in Florida who took us snorkeling. It was crawling along the bottom. They made chowder and we ate it.

Dolly seemed to want to know about everything in the room. Jenny realized she had forgotten about a lot of this stuff some time back.

Suddenly Jenny stopped, distracted by a startling thought.

What? Dolly asked.

Oh my gosh... When I was in Jason's head or self or whatever... I ran into all this stuff. I ran into a lot of bad emotions and hatred and anger; a lot of evil garbage that he's done...

And...? prompted Dolly.

What was weird— what I didn't understand was this stuff... It was like a glue, or maybe a thick soup; It was a medium that held all the bad stuff together. It connected all the fear, the hatred, and the bad experiences. It was like a damaged circuit board, designed to think crazy thoughts, and it seems to feed off the person. I just realized what the stuff is...

Dolly patiently waited for Jenny to continue.

It's drugs. It's drugs the psychiatrists give him— all these psychiatric drugs, lots of them. That's what immersed him in the evil. He's insane, and they did that to him.

*   *   *

It was a warm Saturday afternoon. Jenny's attention was distracted by laughter wafting up from the backyard. She paused and listened to the musical quality of the sound. She went to the open window, knelt on the carpet and looked down.

Her mother was sitting in the gazebo, sipping coffee, listening to Dolly's stories of life in New England back in the 18ᵗʰ century. Jenny could see they were becoming very close. *They get to play and I get to do homework.*

But her time with Dolly was after dark when they would venture into the night on various adventures while her body was asleep in her bed, reminiscent of the coma that held it prisoner for months. They spent some time together during the day, but it was their nocturnal adventures she appreciated the most.

The amount of time she spent on homework had increased lately since Thaddeus had instilled in Jenny a fascination for words and their meanings. She had discovered the joy of thought; unencumbered thought, born of understanding. And the more words she really understood, the greater was her understanding of the world around her.

"Words mean things…," Jenny muttered to herself. It sounded so stupid as she said it aloud but the simplicity and understanding that she got from that silly realization went far beyond the mere concept that the statement held.

Then she realized that words were merely the expression of thought. Thought fascinated her. *You get a con-cept, an idea and that is thought. People can think won-derful things; that's where all beautiful poetry, music, and art come from.*

Jenny thought of Jason. The more Jenny became fas-cinated with thought and words, the more she wondered about Jason and his thinking and his attitude. His thought, his thinking he thinks in dark concepts and angry emotion. And he doesn't understand the meanings of words.

But she knew Jason. He wasn't always like that. She could very easily recall the happy, funny kid she had spent the early years of her childhood with. She wanted to help him, but felt powerless in the face of the mental and spiritual corruption that seemed to rule him.

I would find him again. She laid on her bed, gave a sigh and relaxed.

She found him playing video games with Bobby, in the basement of what was probably Bobby's house. Bobby was intent on the game he was involved in. Jason lit a ciga-rette and laid back into the stuffed chair. She settled softly, carefully around him.

Oh, if Dolly finds out she will be SO angry with me! I'll go lightly...

* * *

Jenny was sitting on her bed thinking about recent events, when Dolly appeared.

You're depressed..., Dolly said.

She looked into Dolly's eyes. At first, there was a flicker of irritation, almost anger that turned to disappointment. She didn't know which was worse.

You went there the first time and got pulled into God knows what, Dolly said. *You went there again and I find you sitting here in this depression. It's icky...*

I wanted to help him, she replied sadly. *I don't know what to do. If you could see what he was like when he was little...*

He's not little and he's not like that anymore, Dolly said. *I think he's dangerous and I'm worried about you. He's being evil and evil is infectious; I can already see the effect this is having on you. And then it can infect me and your mother and your little sisters. That is how evil spreads. It's like a disease that goes from person to person.*

That scares me when you say that, Jenny replied. *I don't ever want to do anything bad to you or to my family.*

Well, this scares me, Dolly said. *I saw what I had to pull you out of the other day. That boy is insane. Are you playing the moth to the candle?*

No, Jenny said, looking down. *I won't go back there, I promise.*

Dolly smiled and her eyes softened.

It's drugs, Jenny said. *It's drugs that did this to him! They have him on about six different drugs. They made him like this. He might have been confused and troubled, but those evil drugs given to him by evil people, made him worse, much worse.*

*   *   *

She's right! Thaddeus barked. *Be thankful you are blest with such friends. I've watched drugs ruin education over the years. Drugs and psychiatry; they go hand in hand. These charlatans set up a psychiatric bureaucracy in our schools. And that bureaucracy is nothing more than a drug distribution system that has flooded the schools with their prescription drugs. Drug use and education are not compatible. As drug use increased in our schools, education decreased. Good education has become the exception rather than the rule.*

Yes, I could see that in Bobby as well as Jason, Jenny said. *They're pretty ruined. And I don't see how this damage will ever be undone. Even if the boys stopped using drugs, I seriously doubt that their ability to think properly will ever be rehabilitated. You could get the drugs out of the body, but not out of the mind.*

It was the next day and Jenny was sitting on her bed. A gentle breeze flowed into the room through the open window.

How are you doing now? Dolly said.

Good. I'm done with all that.

The thing with Jason?

Yeah, Jenny said a she shrugged her shoulders. *I learned about evil.*

Dolly raised her eyebrows, questioningly.

Yeah, Jenny said, *Evil comes from corrupted thought.*

136

All of life comes from thought. When thought is corrupted, life becomes corrupted. Crime, perversion, suffering it all comes from corrupted thought. Drugs pervert and corrupt thought. They create false joy that eventually becomes suffering. I'll never take drugs, Jenny said.

*　　*　　*

~ 5 ~

History and Psychiatry

Jenny's favorite subject was history. When she studied it, she could clearly envision the events she read about. She was determined to learn true history, not the fake history that Thaddeus disparaged so ruthlessly. He was over 250 years old! And Dolly was almost that old. Between the two of them, she had access to a lot of history!

Her history teacher was named Mrs. Lewiston. She always seemed very bitter; but she did appreciate history, and as Jenny sat in the class listening to her discuss historical events, her spirits would lift. As she looked out the window, she could feel herself lift away above the trees. When they spoke of the Battle of Bunker Hill, she found herself looking down on Breed's Hill over in Charleston. *This was where it happened. Boston is so full of history!*

One afternoon, they were discussing the early days of the Revolutionary War. She found herself slipping back to the Boston Common in the 1770s. Boston was so different then; she could see the magnificent sailing ships in Boston Harbor, and it was a short walk to where the Boston Tea Party happened.

Suddenly her reverie was broken by Mrs. Lewiston speaking to her sharply.

"Jenny! Are you even paying attention to what we are

discussing here? Are you interested at all?"

"Yes, ma'am, very much so," Jenny insisted.

"I think you need to come see me after class."

Jenny was stunned. *What did I do? Why would she want to see me? Am I in trouble?*

Eventually, the class ended, and Jenny approached her desk.

"Jenny, have a seat," Mrs. Lewiston said, pointing to a desk in the front row. When Jenny was seated, she continued.

"I'm concerned about your participation in this class," she said sternly.

Jenny was surprised and didn't know what to say.

"During the lessons, I often see you staring out the window or daydreaming. I'm very concerned about this."

"I understand the lessons," Jenny said defensively. "I do all my homework, and I get all A's on my tests. I love history."

"Jenny, I have no complaints about your academic abilities. I understand that you're one of the smartest students in the school. That's why I'm concerned; I'm very concerned about *you*, Jenny."

"I don't understand," Jenny said.

"It's most often our brightest students who are the ones experiencing the most difficulties in their lives. I think you're very unhappy and you need to get help."

Jenny was stunned. "I'm not unhappy, Mrs. Lewiston. I don't understand"

"I've been watching you for a while, Jenny. You spend a

lot of time staring out the window and being very distract-ed in class. You may be a straight-A student, but your aca-demic record is not necessarily an indicator of how you are really doing. This is a common problem with our brightest students. We constantly have to intervene on their behalf."

Jenny didn't know how to respond.

"I'm scheduling an appointment for you with one of our counselors. She will assist you with the things that are causing you to be so unhappy. She can help you."

*　　*　　*

Jenny really didn't understand why any of this was happening. As she entered the counseling office, a woman with a severe look on her face pointed to a chair and said, "Have a seat, I'll be with you in a moment." She went into another office and closed the door.

Fifteen minutes later, the woman came out of the office and stood in front of her.

"Are you Jenny?" she asked.

"Yes, ma'am," she replied.

"Come in my office, and we'll start."

Jenny followed her into the office and sat where the woman indicated.

"Jenny, what we need to do is determine why you're so unhappy and prescribe a remedy for whatever that is."

Over the next half hour, the woman questioned her about many areas of her life, asking her how she felt about this and how she felt about that. Jenny was alarmed and didn't trust this woman.

"Jenny, I think we have a serious situation here. I think you're bipolar and need some help rather urgently. I've written this prescription for you. Take it to your mother. Tell her she must fill it immediately and follow the directions on the label."

Jenny didn't remember the names of the drugs that the woman told her she was prescribing. Her instinct told her that something was very wrong with this. With apprehension churning her stomach, she left the office.

*   *   *

Her mother stared down at the scribbled prescription.

"I don't understand, Mommy. I'm not confused, I'm not unhappy. I love history! Mrs. Lewiston doesn't understand at all. I do all my homework; I get really good grades! And drugs! Why do they want me to take drugs??? That's what ruined Jason!"

"Jason Brenner?" her mother asked.

"Yes, and he's so changed. He's so unhappy and a little scary. He hangs around with Bobby Roland, and they're both on a lot of drugs. And they're crazy!"

I made a mistake once, Janice thought. I let Agnes interfere with me and my daughter, and I almost lost her. This is dangerous. My daughter is not confused, she's not unhappy. She's an extremely well-adjusted girl.

There is no way in hell I will allow this to happen.

*   *   *

"What are you attempting here and why?"

Jenny's mother was sitting across from the Thayer

school assistant principal.

"We are not attempting anything here. We are charged with overseeing not only the children's education but their well-being. Our staff are trained to detect problems and situations with our students, and we employ established remedies."

"What problem or 'situation' are you attempting to remedy here?" Janice asked.

"Mrs. Lewiston observed classroom behavior that greatly concerned her. She had her see one of our counselors, and her concerns were found to be correct."

"What behavior? She's one of the most brilliant students in your school. Her IQ is off the charts. She's never failed to turn in an assignment, and from what I understand, she has never gotten a question wrong on a test. Why would you even bother a child like this?"

"Research has shown that the brightest students are the ones that most easily mask deep-seated frustration and problems," the assistant principal said. "Also, Jenny has no really close friends in this school."

"That is because Jenny isn't into what a lot of the students in this school are into," her mother said. "She isn't into smoking or body piercing or tattoos or dyeing her hair purple. She wants no part of the dangerous sexual status quo that is prevalent in middle schools. She finds drug use abhorrent. And you want to change that. You have a number of very confused children in your school who are into extremely dangerous conduct. Yet, you prefer to attack one of your most stable students!"

"We are not attacking this girl. We want to help her," he said indignantly.

"This is not help! There is no way I will allow you to put my daughter on drugs."

"Then," he paused for dramatic effect. "She will not be allowed to attend this school or any public school in this county until she complies with this order."

"No, you can't do that," she said. "This is stupid, destructive behavior. You're failing to educate or to help these children. And in the death throes of your own competence and integrity, you've chosen to harm them!"

*   *   *

"You won't be attending school for a while," her mother said. "I've arranged for Chatan to return, and your education will continue uninterrupted. I went and talked with the assistant principal and the counselor, and they couldn't give me any good reasons for targeting you. Furthermore, they said that if you didn't take their drugs, you can't attend school. The school board refused to even take my complaint."

"Earlier today, I went and saw a lawyer," she continued. "We're suing the school, the school board, Mrs. Lewiston, and the school counselor. There is no way I'm going to allow this."

"Isn't it expensive to sue them?" Jenny asked.

"We can afford it. The settlement from your accident was quite generous. And this is quite important. And we are suing for court costs. Our lawyer has handled this type of thing a lot, and he is quite sure it may not cost us anything."

"OK," Jenny said.

"I'm just glad Dolly doesn't go to school," her mother added.

*   *   *

Jenny and her mother sat across the desk from their lawyer.

"Jenny," he said as he rose from the chair and extended his hand. "I've been looking forward to meeting you," he said.

"Don't let this worry you. We're in an advantageous position here. The normal procedure is to have you be interviewed by a psychiatrist of our choosing, but I'm going to have you do an interview with three psychiatrists. That will leave no room for dispute. These are guys I work with all the time. They're good guys and they deal with younger people on a regular basis."

"Do we go to court?" Jenny asked.

"Yes. They may offer to withdraw the order and allow you back in school, but that's not what we want. I'm also concerned that there may be repercussions when you get back to school. I want to take this into court and get a ruling barring this order as well as prevent any repercussions."

"But another thing I'm concerned with is that you understand that there is nothing wrong with you. These are vicious people who do a lot of damage to children, mostly to very bright students like yourself. Are we good?" he asked, smiling.

"Yeah," she said. She was relieved, and she really trusted this lawyer.

* * *

~ 6 ~

The Old and the New

Jenny and Janice were sitting with Thaddeus and Dolly on a picnic bench outside the school beneath a massive tree that created a comfortable shade all around them.

The problem is drugs, Thaddeus said, *and the people who push them into our schools.*

Playful noise drifted across the playground from a baseball diamond where a girls' softball game was going on.

How did this all happen? her mother asked.

After World War II, they slowly started building a psychiatric bureaucracy in the schools, Thaddeus said. Since then, it has grown and never stopped growing in size or influence. That bureaucracy was put there to introduce psychiatric drugs into the schools. It is entrenched in these schools like a cancer.

Why? Jenny asked.

Greed, mostly, he said. *To understand this, you must first come to terms with the fact that there are evil people in the world. And there are people who appease evil people. There is considerable money made from drugging children. The drug companies are some of the biggest corporations in the world, and their influence is extensive. They are unconcerned about the damage they do.*

This is mind-boggling, her mother said.

He turned to Jenny. *You mentioned your childhood friend, Jason. You spoke of how he seemed very dark and that he scared you. That is the type of damage they do. I've watched that boy go from a normal student to a dark, moody boy who is, in my opinion, dangerous. It's the drugs that made him like that.*

How do you understand all of this? her mother asked. *You lived more than two hundred years ago.*

Yes, but I didn't stop observing when I passed, and I didn't stop learning. Dolly, as far as I can tell, passed sometime in the 1780s, yet she knows about automobiles and jet planes and knows what computers are. We observe the culture; we have a full library here and I have read several thousand books since I passed.

Dolly and Thaddeus were gone. Jenny and her mother were walking toward the car as the last bit of dusk became the night.

"You have some interesting friends, sweetheart," her mother said.

"Wait until you meet Malcolm," Jenny replied.

*   *   *

The full moon illuminated the row of houses beneath them. Jenny was gazing at the brightly lit skyscrapers of Boston. She found the Public Garden with the antique-style lamp posts; beyond it, the Common was a dark patch. When she was out of her body, her vision was considerably better than when she was using her eyes. Being able to see things clearly at great distance, even in the dark, was quite normal.

Suddenly the brightly lit city of Boston stretched out below them.

The Back Bay, Dolly said, pointing, *was under water. I watched it grow from a colonial city to this. The original city was called Shawmut. It was on a peninsula connected to the mainland by a thin strip of land. They cut down some of the hills and filled in the bay. I watched them build the expressways and the Turnpike.*

When was that?

The expressways? They started building them in the 1950s and have been ever since. And then they had the Big Dig.

Wow, Jenny said. *I never realized that; you've been in this area for over two hundred years. I mean, I realized it, but I never thought...*

Yes, Dolly said. *You see the big glass mirror windows on the John Hancock Tower? All of the windows shattered during the construction of the building; the falling glass became a danger to cars as well as pedestrians.*

All of them? Jenny asked, *at once?*

All of them, but it happened over many months; some broke twice. They built wooden platforms on four sides of the building above the streets. At one point, there were so many windows boarded up, the locals called it the 'plywood skyscraper'.

Jenny said nothing as she thoughtfully gazed at the glass tower.

It was built right beside the Trinity Church, Dolly

continued. *This was a beautiful, historic landmark built right after the Civil War. I believe it stressed the foundation of the church, and they had to pay millions of dollars in damages.*

Why did the windows fall out? Jenny asked.

I guess originally the windows were designed, manufactured or installed incorrectly, but after a while, I think there were ghosts playing pranks, which made it go on for a long time.

Ghosts? Jenny asked.

Yes, sometimes they pull pranks like that. But it's usually against someone who got them upset. Maybe they were kicked out of the buildings that were torn down to make way for the big building.

A modern version of a haunted house, Jenny said.

Yes! Dolly said, laughing.

*   *   *

I want to ask you something, Jenny said cautiously.

What?

Jenny hesitated. *Can I see your grave? I want to see your tombstone. I used to walk around the graveyard and read the tombstones and think about the people. But I never found yours. And I looked.*

Dolly got a sad look. *Yes.*

We don't have to...

No, it's OK..., Come.

Dolly led her to a far section in the northeast corner. It was overgrown; some of the stones were crooked, and a couple were knocked over. Jenny saw one tombstone at a weird angle in a bush.

They stood where the freshly cut, beautifully mani-cured grass ended, and the rough grass and brush began. Two feet in was a tombstone that had sunk into the dirt and was standing at a severe angle. Jenny looked closely at the stone. She could make out the words Dolores Erin Cla-hane. There was a date below it, but it was partially buried and obscured.

Oh... Jenny said.

Yes. It just keeps getting worse over the years. I hav-en't been here in a long time. I just stopped coming...

Wow, I'm sorry, Jenny said.

*   *   *

~ 7 ~

Stand Your Ground

The school's lawyer called the counselor to the stand.

"Could you give the court your evaluation of this child?"

"Well, after interviewing her teacher and speaking to the girl, I ran her through a standard evaluation questionnaire. I determined that she was exhibiting bipolar and ADHD manifestations."

"What were those manifestations?" he asked.

"She tends to disassociate. She has delusional tendencies."

"How? Could you tell the court more about that?"

"Well, one thing is when the teacher is lecturing, the child goes into delusional projections about the lesson."

"Really?" the lawyer asked. "What does this mean?"

"Well, she is disassociating. She loses touch with the real world."

Jenny was uncomfortable as the counselor droned on; she tuned out. Her attention returned to the front of the courtroom when the lawyer thanked the counselor and ended.

Her lawyer waived the cross-examination.

The school's lawyer called her teacher.

"Mrs. Lewiston, what behavior on Jenny's part did you observe that prompted you to send her to the counselor?"

"When I was lecturing, she would be staring off into space. I would often see her daydreaming."

"And this raised concerns on your part?" he asked.

"Yes, we have a set of guidelines that we go by. Our policy is that when we see these types of manifestations, we send her to see one of the counselors."

Jenny tuned out again. She really didn't want to listen to them talk about her like that.

He ended off and it was her lawyer's turn. He got up to cross-examine her.

"Is Jenny a good student?"

"Well, she exhibits tendencies..."

"I did not ask you that. Does she do all of her assignments? How does she do on tests? Does she get things wrong on tests?"

"Well, no, she does quite well. She's maintained an A-plus average. I don't think she's ever gotten a question wrong on a test."

"Oh?" the lawyer asked, surprised.

"No, her academic abilities are not the problem. She's actually quite brilliant," the counselor said apologetically. "It's our brightest students who have the greatest problems socially and psychologically."

"Does she act out in class?"

"No..."

Is she a discipline problem?"

"No."

"Tardy? Chronic absenteeism?"

"No."

"Conflict with other students or staff?"

"No."

"Is she suspected of substance abuse?"

"No."

"Does she act out in a self -destructive manner?"

"Well, no. But we are trained to recognize certain warning signs in our students. And we act on those. Socially, she is disconnected from the rest of the student body. She has no close friends that we could discover."

"OK," the lawyer said. "Do you have discipline problems in your school?"

"Considerable problems, like any public school," she answered.

"Promiscuity? Teen pregnancy?" he asked.

"Yes," she replied.

"Illegal drug use?"

"Yes, a good amount," she said.

"Violence?"

"Y-yes..."

"Well, why haven't you handled it?"

"We are understaffed and underfunded. We don't have the resources to handle..."

"So, it seems as if your school environment is very problematic, almost out of control."

"Well, that's a bit..."

"Why would any normal, bright girl want to be a part of this? It sounds to me like she avoids a lot of problems such as drugs, promiscuity, and violence. Isn't it true that instead of getting involved in all these situations at the school, she puts all of her attention into her schoolwork and into getting an education?"

"Yes, but that's not always healthy."

He glanced at her questioningly; after a moment he continued.

"You mentioned daydreaming..." he said.

"Yes, it occurs quite regularly."

"What was she daydreaming about?" he asked her.

"I don't know. There's no way for me to know that."

"Did you ask her?"

"Well... no. It's not my job to..."

"It isn't?" the lawyer cut her off.

"Well, no... I"

"That will be all. Thank you."

Jenny's lawyer called her to the stand.

"Jenny, are you unhappy?"

"No. I'm not."

"I imagine it's hard to prove something like that," he said. "Tell me about school. Do you like school?"

"Oh yes! I love learning; I love knowing about things. I love history and I love grammar and English. I have a friend, who is the smartest man I know. He constantly tells me about the importance of studying history and really knowing the definitions of words. And he is so right. Now, I learn my definitions and it is so easy to learn other subjects when you do this."

"Tell me about any problems you've had with history class. You told me that you love history, and I see that you get all A's, but Mrs. Lewiston says you have problems, that you get distracted and daydream."

"No, no..." she said, looking very thoughtful.

"Do you stare out the window a lot?"

"Well... yes."

"Tell me about that. Why do you daydream? What do you daydream about?"

"Well... she talks to us about history. She tells about battles and moving west to settle the country, and fur trappers and riverboats. And I listen, and I can see it in front of me. I can see the battles; I can see covered wagons and sailing ships and the building of the railroad and it's wonderful. And it helps me to know so much about it. I'm not unhappy in class; I'm learning and I love to learn."

"Hmmm," the lawyer said. "Tell me about your life at home. How is that? Your father is gone? How do you and your mother get along?"

"My father died right after my youngest sisters were born. I miss him, but there's nothing I can do about that, so I just moved on. My mother is one of my best friends. She has four little girls and me. And she does really well. When I was in the hospital, she came every day and read to me even though I was in a coma. I have my own room at home, and I love my little sisters, and I take responsibility for them."

"What is the biggest concern in your life?" he asked.

"I want to do more for my mother. She does really well, but I... I kind of forget sometimes how hard she works; sometimes I take her for granted and it makes me feel bad," she said.

"And how do you handle that?" he asked.

"Well, I used to go and ask her what I could help her with, but she would say that she's fine. Then..." she drew out the word for effect. "Then, I stopped asking her. I watched her. And she would say something like, 'Oh, I forgot to feed the twins,' and I would say, 'I can feed them!' and I would. And that worked out really good or... well, I should say it worked out really well."

"Is there anything you want to say to the court?"

"I don't understand why this happened. And I don't understand why they wanted me to take drugs. I never miss school, I'm never late. I do all my homework. I have the best grades in school. I never get in trouble. I don't understand why they feel they need to 'fix' me. I'm not broken!"

"My friend Jason, they put him on a bunch of different drugs, and he's not the same. He's moody and he's dark and very unhappy. He used to be my childhood friend, but now he scares me."

"The fact that they want to put me on drugs makes me unhappy. They should only do that when they really have to. I don't need any drugs, and I don't understand why they insisted. They kicked me out of school!"

"I understand," he said. "That will be all, Jenny. Thank you."

The school's lawyer had no questions.

One by one, their lawyer called his psychiatrists. Their testimony was good. All three of them agreed that Jenny was a very well-adjusted, stable girl, and there is no reason at all why she should be put on the drugs especially as a requirement to attend school.

The school's lawyer stood.

"Your Honor, could we have a thirty-minute recess?"

"Thirty minutes," the judge said as he tapped his gavel and stood up.

*   *   *

"She is killing us," the lawyer said.

He was standing with the assistant principal, the counselor, and Mrs. Lewiston.

"This is not some scared little girl that was on the stand. Three psychiatrists!" he said with exasperation. "She put the coffin lid on this case, and they nailed it shut."

"What do you think we should do?" asked the assistant principal.

"I'm going to go to her lawyer and offer to rescind the drug requirement order if he'll drop the suit."

Jenny and her mother were approached by their lawyer. Dolly was somewhere around, poking into things.

"Their lawyer has offered to rescind the drug requirement order and allow her to return to school if we will drop the lawsuit. I told him no. They're not in a good position. Our three experts, as well as Jenny's testimony, destroyed their case. I want a ruling on this, and I want court costs. I want this to be on their dime. And I want to cost them some money. I run into this all the time and this..., well, never mind."

"I agree, totally," her mother said.

The bailiff came out and herded them all back into

the courtroom.

"Your Honor," her lawyer said. "I'm asking the court to declare the requirement that this child be put on medication in order to attend school be made null and void."

"Their actions were arbitrary and capricious and put this child's education at risk. This single mother was forced to great effort to defend this child against this overwhelming bureaucratic bullying. This child is a model student; her academic record is the best in the school. By their testimony, she is not a disciplinary problem, yet they chose to target her. They claimed that she was unhappy. It seems the only unhappiness that this girl was experiencing was caused by the school. They said that she was guilty of daydreaming. Yet, they never even questioned her about what was happening. It seems her 'daydreaming' assisted her in learning the subject and retaining what she learned. This girl has not been a problem to anyone, yet she was singled out and bullied by personnel at this school."

"I'm asking for court costs and tutoring costs, as well as $100,000 in mental suffering. I'm also requesting a restraining order against the school, the school board, and any of its personnel to ensure there are no repercussions regarding this matter. Upon that, I rest my case. Thank you."

Jenny listened as the school's lawyer argued their position. She soon got bored with it and found Dolly hovering near the clock. Her mother looked up at her and smiled, and then smiled at Jenny, as the judge called a recess and went into his chambers.

*   *   *

An hour later, the bailiff recalled their case.

The judge settled in his chair and then everyone else did the same. He organized some papers and then spoke.

"The school overstepped their boundaries when they barred the child from attending school. I don't see that the school had any justified basis for requiring the child to take medication. I think the school board was culpable when they refused the plaintiff's request for appeal; they supported the school's decision."

"They did interrupt her education and caused the mother to have to hire a tutor. The school acted contrary to the best interests of the child and her education."

"I'm declaring the medical requirement for attending school null and void. I am issuing an order of restraint against the defendants regarding this child. The school, as well as the school board, will be liable for court costs, tutoring expenses, as well as $50,000 for mental suffering."

He brought down his gavel and dismissed the court.

"Wow," her lawyer said as he turned to her mother, "I'm sorry."

"About what?" her mother asked. "We won."

"I really thought I could get you that $100,000."

*   *   *

~ 8 ~

The Graveyard

Jenny was ignored in school, for the most part, which allowed her to pursue her education which was exactly what she wanted.

Remarkably, Mrs. Lewiston accepted the outcome of the suit. It seemed as if she left it behind and decided that Jenny was her student, and it was her job to get Jenny through the school year which was actually, remarkably easy. The school counselor seemed to pretend that Jenny was invisible

Jenny saw Jason around the school. She would say hello as they passed, but it was limited to that, except that she could see the uneasiness and discomfort that would take hold of him when she looked into his eyes.

*   *   *

"This is a beautiful place," Janice said. "I had forgotten. I haven't been here since we laid your father to rest years ago."

"I have about a dozen friends in this graveyard," Jenny said. "Two years ago, I started coming here. Do you remember when Jeremy was killed?"

"Clearly," her mother said.

"That's where they found his body," Jenny said, pointing. "I was coming here almost every night until the street-

160

lights came on."

Her mother looked surprised.

"I just want to tell you everything; I don't want any more secrets. The reason Jeremy was killed was that he knew I was coming in here and was determined to find out what I was doing. And all that time, the creepy man was stalking me; he was following me."

"But Jeremy was following me also. The night he was killed, the creepy man was waiting in here for me but my friends, the ghosts, wouldn't let me in. But they didn't stop Jeremy and the creepy man found him and killed him."

Jenny sighed and looked away, visualizing Jeremy's death.

"You knew the creepy man was stalking you and you still came here regularly?" her mother asked.

"No. I knew he was dangerous, and one night I thought he was looking for me, but I didn't know he was stalking me. I thought he was just another creep who liked to make trouble, like Jeremy. I didn't know he would hurt me."

"That scares me, quite a bit," her mother said.

"Well, there's a dozen ghosts who never would have let him hurt me. But there is someone I want you to meet."

*   *   *

She walked over to a bench and sat down; her mother sat beside her. After a minute, a tall, elderly Black man approached them; from where, her mother wasn't sure.

Malcolm, Jenny said as she stood. *I want you to meet someone; have a seat.*

I appreciate, he said as he sat beside her mother.

This is Janice, my mother, she said proudly.

Pleased to make your acquaintance, the ghost said, removing his hat, *very pleased. Dolly told me 'bout how you've taken her under your wing.*

I'm very glad to meet you, her mother said. *Jenny told me so much about you. And yes, Dolly's a really good girl. We're proud to make her a member of our family. We love her so much.*

I was so happy to hear that, he said. *It's a good thing you done. She's been wandering around here alone, for nigh on two hundred years. That is, until Jenny comes along. I think she been around longer than any of us.*

She spoke to me of the hours she spent listening to your tales of the railroad, her mother said. *How long did you work for them?*

Well, ma'am, I started with the railroad when I was but a boy. I was still working for them at my demise, which near as I can remember was 1910; it's on my stone here, somewhere.

How old were you at the time? her mother asked.

I don't rightly know. I was passin' for a man when Mr. Lincoln's War broke out. I was smuggled up here on the Underground Railroad when I was about twelve. Near as I can figure, I was born about 1840. So, I imagine that I was seventy when I passed.

You knew Harriet Tubman? her mother asked.

Nooo, she came 'long way after me. A preacher taught me to read and write and got me a job on the railroad for a penny a day, and I never left. I never had money 'fore that. For twenty years, I didn't have a home. I was happy to live on the train. Then one day I moved into an abandoned caboose on an old siding. I dragged an old stove in there and put up a flue.

A flue? Jenny asked.

Chimney, he said.

What did you do on the railroad?

Most everything mostly shoveled coal to keep the boiler going. But it was good work, and I was a free man, he said proudly.

You liked that work?

The Lord blessed me when he sent one of His servants to help me get that job. I've been all over this country many times.

*   *   *

The sun was low on the horizon as Jenny and her mother continued through the graveyard.

"What did you want to show me?"

"We're almost there."

They stopped at a remote section of the graveyard, a forgotten corner where brush obscured some of the graves and the grass was overgrown. Some were missing headstones, and a number were knocked over or sat at a weird angle.

Jenny showed her one grave with a tilted headstone. She squatted down to see the name. In the waning light, the name 'Dolores Erin Clahane' was visible.

"Oh my!" her mother said. "This is ... Wow, this is not good. I feel sorry for her. Does she feel bad about this?"

"Yeah... more than she will admit; she never comes here anymore. Tombstones are a bit of a status thing among ghosts. The ones in the center of the graveyard with statues and such—those ghosts are insufferable."

*   *   *

~ 9 ~

Tragedy at Thayer

Life returned to normal or as normal as it could be with a girl who was a skilled medium, whose best friends were ghosts, and who could leave her body and roam the environment with her best friend who, as we have come to know, is also a ghost.

One day the school security guard approached Jenny. His name was Adam, and he was a huge, friendly man with a shaved head.

"You're the girl who sued the school when they tried to put you on drugs, aren't you?" he asked.

She nodded her head.

"Good! You're my hero," he said as he held out his hand to shake hers. "They'd rather drug kids than talk to them. And the drugs ruin these kids. They either become more of a problem or they become walking vegetables. They never had the school shootings until they had the drugs!"

"My mother is the hero," Jenny explained as her hand disappeared in his. "I'm not; she fought the fight. They tangled with the wrong mom when they came after me."

"I'd like to be your friend. If you ever need anything, you just ask."

They became close friends. She was interested in his stories of when he was in the military. He was in a special unit of fierce, very skilled fighters. They would send them in to do important, secret things that never got on the news. There were some things he couldn't tell her about, and there were some exciting things he could tell her about but he couldn't say where they happened.

Jenny loved making new friends, and she made some good ones.

*   *   *

One day she arrived at school, and something was different. There was a tension in the air, and she could see that Adam had also picked it up. He seemed to be everywhere at once.

She had just come out of her second-period English class. Two girls ran past her.

"There's two guys over there with guns!" they screamed as they ran for the door.

Two more students ran by yelling, "Guns! Down there!" They pointed in the opposite direction.

In here! It was Thaddeus, pointing toward a closet door. *Lock it when you get inside!*

Jenny ducked into the closet, closed the heavy metal door, and threw the deadbolt.

With her body safe in the janitor's closet, she was free to take to the sky above the school; she saw dozens of students pouring from the building. Then she was in one of the corridors. She saw Bobby and Jason as they came around a corner. They were both heavily armed, each with two pistols; Jason had a rifle over one shoulder. They both wore heavy coats with big pockets.

Jenny pushed her way into Jason's head. His anger was now a suppressed rage, and he was intent on hurting people. Then she saw something that made her chill. Somehow, they had gotten a brick of plastic explosive. Jason had the trigger in one of those big pockets in that heavy jacket, and they were looking for a place to plant it.

Where do two fifteen-year-old boys get plastic explosive???

They were walking down the corridor, about thirty feet from where Jenny's body was hidden in the closet. She was stunned as she returned to her body.

I have to do something! I don't know…

She found herself turning the deadbolt and stepping into the corridor. She would confront Jason; there was no way he was going to do this thing.

When she locked eyes with him, she knew she had him.

She poured joyful memories into him—the years of fun they had together, the amazing times they had. They were running up and down the beach, they were playing in the bubbling stream behind their house. They were spacemen; they were sailors; they were cowboys and Indians.

With every bit of moral, mental, and spiritual strength that she had, she took hold of him. He wasn't going to do this. She was going to find that happy little boy again.

As he looked at her, his bearing faltered; she was reaching him.

"Jason, don't do this…" she implored as his face distorted into a look of horror.

Bobby turned toward her and raised his pistol.

"Shut the hell up!" he roared.

*　　*　　*

Adam turned toward two of the male teachers, who were looking to him for orders.

"Get as many students out of the school as you can. Tell them just keep running but not so fast that they will fall. Get as many as you can out, staying as long as you dare, then get out yourself!"

He turned toward the students running toward them.

"Where are they?" he yelled.

"Over by the chemistry lab!"

He drew his pistol and headed in that direction.

A girl ran by him, pointing. He turned a corner and spotted them. It was Jason and Bobby; he knew them both well and feared that this day would come. Jenny was facing both of them. He got the idea that the brave little fool was trying to stop them.

Bobby yelled at Jenny to shut the hell up and raised his gun.

*　　*　　*

When Jason faltered, she knew she could stop him; he looked ashamed and embarrassed. But then an angry look returned to his face.

Then the bullets from Bobby's gun tore into her lungs. Her body toppled to the floor, blood spurting from its chest. She stared down in disbelief at the blood-stained body lying below her. She felt bad that it had ruined her favorite outfit. She watched as Jason angrily raised his pistol and shot Bobby in the forehead. He died instantly, as his body fell to the floor a few feet from her body.

She glanced toward movement at the end of the corridor as Adam raised his pistol and shot Jason dead.

*　　*　　*

~ 10 ~

Aftermath

Over a thousand people attended the funeral.

The newspapers called her a hero— the 14-year-old, A-plus female student who gave her life to save the school and the other students. But after two days, it had all become just a lot of noise that Janice struggled to get away from.

The security guard insisted on taking her to the funeral. He had introduced himself on the day of the shooting. His name was Adam, and he said that he and Jenny were good friends; Janice recalled her mentioning him.

"I appreciate all your help, but you haven't slept in two days. I think I can handle the rest from here."

"No, ma'am," he said solemnly. "She's gone; that's on me. I've seen a lot of war and a lot of violence, and somehow, I've managed to keep my soul intact. But if I don't do everything I can to help you and your family, if I don't do everything I can to make this easy on you and help you get through this, I don't think I will ever be comfortable with myself again."

So, he was there, constantly helping her through the painful procedures and the constant barrage of unwelcome press that accompanied this tragedy. People didn't get very pushy with him.

But right now, she was having trouble standing. He put

his massive hands on her shoulder and held her up. After again apologizing for his failure to save Jenny, he simply joined her in her grief.

"For all that we have been through, despite what she went through at the hospital, I still lost her!"

Her grief weighed so heavily in her throat and chest she could barely function.

She turned to Adam. "This is not right! There is no justice in this world when someone like her is taken. She was fourteen years old!"

Adam struggled to contain his grief but failed; he simply stood there holding her. Tears flowed down his face and dampened his uniform as they lowered the casket into the ground. He really liked that little girl.

He raised his head. He had failed but he would face the consequences and be there for her mother and family.

As he watched the casket disappear into the ground, he noticed a new tombstone on the grave to the right of hers. This was the oldest section of the graveyard, but the new tombstone matched the one that would go on Jenny's grave. It had the name Dolores Erin Clahane freshly carved in the marble.

*   *   *

It was several days before Janice could bear to even open the door to her room. As she stumbled into the room, her grief returned. She sat on the bed and picked up a stuffed animal that Jenny's father had given her when she was four.

The memories of Jenny's life poured through her grief.

I can give away some..., but she couldn't; she could barely enter the room.

I have four more girls! she told herself. *They need me; they need me more than ever!*

But it hurt so bad. *Janice, get yourself together!*

Two days later she returned.

I've got to confront this, she told herself. *Stop being stupid, Janice. She would tell you to stop being a victim!*

She stood two feet inside the room. She looked across at the new winter jacket she had recently gotten for her. She shook her head sadly. Then she noticed that it still had the tag on it; Jenny had never even worn it.

Well, that's an easy one; back to the store.

There was that cross-country trophy. There were certificates of accomplishment in various areas, framed and hung on the walls.

I should get Wendy to come in and help; it's going to be her room.

She looked at the bookcase. Jenny didn't just have books sitting there each one was very special to her. There were hairclips sitting on her vanity, along with a brush.

She went to the garage, got a plastic leaf bag, and returned to the room. She dropped the hairbrush and the hairclips in. She realized that she should just find things that had no emotional attachment and get rid of those.

She went to the desk and pulled a drawer open. There was a bunch of letters and things she had written. There were a lot of things that would be important to Jenny but to no one else.

She imagined time as a stream flowing through the room. She imagined herself taking things and throwing them into that stream—things that would just flow away to be forgotten. It somehow made it easier. She was moving through the room, finding things that could go.

There was some nice sketching that Jenny had done. She had some talent. *She should have pursued that...*

She stopped in amazement. That sketching—it was Jenny and Dolly! She had made a perfect sketch of them together. They were hovering over the city skyline. The lower parts of their bodies faded to nothing.

Don't be hard on yourself! Jenny scolded. *I don't need this stuff anymore. There are some things that would be nice to keep around, maybe a few favorite things, but you shouldn't make this into a big problem.*

"What?" her mother said aloud as she bent over holding her head; darkness seemed to be closing in around her as she struggled to keep her sanity. She envisioned herself crumpling to the floor; huddled beside the bed until death claimed her suffering.

Don't do this to yourself! Jenny said. *I was never that attached to all my 'stuff.' For you, there's going to be tears and memories in every drawer that you go through. You should just get rid of it and give the room to Wendy.*

"What who..."

Jenny appeared in front of her, still wearing her favorite outfit that she had worn to school that day. It was untouched.

Mommy...

Janice gasped as a hand reached out and squeezed her lungs, and she found that she could no longer breathe. She wondered if her heart was beating; she wondered if she was still alive. As her body sagged, the image reached out to her.

Mommy? It's me.

"How?"

Janice found that she was sitting on the bed without any idea of how she got there. Suddenly the image flowed over her, reached into her, and flowed through her like a warm, loving wind of affection.

"Jenny!" she gasped.

I'm here! I came back. I was confused and lost, and I've been trying to get back for days and finally, Dolly found me.

"She's here?"

Yeah. She wanted to give us a few minutes.

She found herself inside her daughter's embrace as she was surrounded, lifted, and healed. Grief drained from her chest, from her soul. All of the crushing agonies of the last week gently, sweetly evaporated.

"I thought I lost you forever!"

She sat on the bed, in Jenny's embrace, and cried for ten minutes.

"Where's Dolly?" she finally asked.

I'm here. The smiling face appeared.

"I looked for you, Dolly, I really did... I couldn't find you! I thought—"

I was off finding Jenny. It wasn't easy!

"Oh, thank you, Dolly. Thank you for bringing her back!"

You've still got six daughters. We're not going anywhere! Dolly said.

"Oh my gosh, I'm going to have to...," her mother said.

What? Jenny said.

"Oh, what do I do with your room? Do you want—but I don't have to do anything with your stuff! I'll let you decide on everything. That's such a relief!"

Give the room to Wendy. Dolly and I will find a favorite place to hang out. There are a few things I'd like to keep. Maybe you could get that nice open shelf cabinet that's in the garage. The one that has a mirror for a back. Have your handyman hang it in that tiny alcove that you never use just a space for Dolly and me. We'll put a few of my things in there, some of my books, and that will be fine. Let the girls have anything else they want and throw away the rest. You can put my school picture in there and tell people that it's a memorial.

"There is a sketching you did that I'm going to frame and hang in that space," her mother said.

What do we tell the girls? Dolly asked.

Jenny and Janice looked at each other and smiled.

We'll handle that when that day comes, Jenny said.

The End

Tribulations of the Ghost

Trilogy of the Ghosts

Book Three

By

Christopher Mercon

~ 1 ~

Wendy and Dolly

"Oh no!"

Wendy stood at the bottom of the front steps of the school and watched as the last school bus disappeared around the corner. She hated calling her mother when she had situations like this, but there were no good alternatives and it was getting dark.

Things took a turn for the worse when she couldn't find her phone. She stopped rummaging through her purse as she tried to remember where she could have put it. She got a sinking feeling in her stomach as she realized it was sitting on the top shelf of her locker. She had set it there while pulling things out of her purse to deal with some other confusion. She hated when chaos crept into her life.

She was alone, standing in front of the school, and the streetlights had already come on. She walked to the top of the stairs and tried the front door. It was locked. She felt very alone with no ride, no phone, and no good ideas. And the concern she felt was slipping into fear.

What should I do? she asked herself. *I can walk. I'm a teenager now. I'm old enough to walk home in the dark.*

She steeled herself, hugged her purse to her chest, and started down the school driveway. She crossed the street and turned right onto the sidewalk in front of a row of storefronts.

She recognized the two gang members that appeared on the other side of the street. They were both sixteen; one had been kicked out of school; the other had quit when he reached the legal age.

If it were one boy, she would've been concerned but not afraid. She had been training at the local dojo for two years. She was a top athlete in her school and wasn't afraid of any boy. But she saw no way she could handle two. She was a tough girl in school, but she was known for always biting off just a little bit more than she could chew.

As they crossed the street behind her, she could feel their attention. She increased her pace.

Another boy appeared a block ahead, walking toward her. She recognized him as another member of the same gang.

She was terrified. She anxiously glanced around, searching for an alternative route an alley or a doorway to an apartment building but saw nothing. She thought of crossing the street again but realized that would gain her nothing and would take her farther from her house.

She looked behind her, but the boys were nowhere in sight. She relaxed slightly and hurried her pace.

She was a block from the school when both boys stepped out of an alley right in front of her, blocking her path. The third boy was with them.

"Where are you going?" one of them demanded snidely.

"I'm going home. Please leave me alone," she said.

"Want to party?" the other asked.

They blocked her path. She stepped off the sidewalk, trying to walk around them.

"Please let me go," she said. "I need to get home."

"You'll go when we say you can go."

This one was taller than the other two and seemed to be the leader. She was terrified of being raped. *I'm only thirteen years old and I'm...*

"You leave me alone! I don't want to talk to you!" she snapped.

A girl about fifteen years old, with brown hair and a long flowing dress, appeared behind her. She grabbed Wendy's shoulders and turned her around.

Keep walking, she said, as she turned toward the boys.

What is she doing? thought Wendy. *Is she crazy? I can't let her face them alone!*

She stood behind the girl, who was aggressively standing up to the bullies.

She had never seen a look of horror like what suddenly appeared on the faces of those boys. They were frozen in shock. She watched as a dark stain appeared on the crotch of the leader's jeans. He gave out a cry and turned so quickly he stumbled as they fled.

The girl turned to her.

Hi, she said. *You shouldn't be out here, alone, after dark. Are you walking home?*

"What did you do? How"

Cowards and bullies, she said nonchalantly. *When people stand up to them, they cower.*

She wasn't so sure but the girl had such certainty! She

was unafraid. *She must be someone these gang members know,* Wendy thought. *Maybe she's someone's girlfriend, someone they're afraid of.*

"But who are you? You made the big guy piss his pants."

She simply shrugged her shoulders and said, *we need to get you home.*

As they walked, Wendy's fears vanished and she felt lifted. She had a natural affection for this girl and knew she was safe by her side.

*　　*　　*

When they reached Wendy's house, the girl said, *You're OK now,* and turned to leave.

"Who are you?" Wendy asked. "I want to be your friend."

I'm Jenny's best friend. We can be friends, but right now I've gotta go.

Before she could get the girl's name, she vanished into the dark.

How can she be Jenny's best friend? Wendy wondered. *Jenny is gone. Doesn't she know?*

As Wendy closed the front door, her mother came out of the kitchen.

"Where have you been?"

"I was at the school late and I missed the last bus."

"Why didn't you call me?" her mother asked.

"I left my phone in my locker and the front door of the school was locked."

"How did you get home?"

"I walked..."

"Alone? After dark? Why would you?"

"I wasn't alone. This older girl walked home with me. She wasn't afraid of anything! She was so..."

"Who is she?" her mother asked.

"I don't know; she said she knew Jenny."

"Ohhh..."

She could see a light come on in her mother's eyes. "Was she a pretty girl with long brown hair and a long flowing dress?"

"Yes. Do you know who she was?"

"Yeah. She was a friend of your sister's. A good friend."

"I've seen her before," Wendy said, wondering. "Her face is familiar."

"You've seen her before?" her mother asked, surprised.

"Wait a minute..."

Her mother could see Wendy's mind racing.

"Yes!" She strode across the room to the alcove, lifted a framed picture off the wall, and brought it into the light.

"Yes, this is her!" she said, holding up the sketch of Jenny and Dolly in the sky over Boston.

"Who is she?" she asked.

"Her name is Dolly. She was Jenny's best friend. She's like another daughter to me."

"That doesn't make sense," Wendy said. "Why have I never met her? If she was Jenny's best friend, why has she never been to this house?"

"I don't know," her mother said, avoiding the question.

"You'll have to ask her."

*   *   *

Wendy was standing in her new bedroom. The room was freshly painted, with new furniture her mother had encouraged her to choose.

The color was perfect, the trim, the doors, perfect. The carpet was perfect. She knew how to design a room. The closet was huge. She had found the perfect comforter for the queen-size bed.

Her mother appeared behind her.

"Nice," she said.

"I wanted my own room, but not like this," Wendy said sadly. "I miss her so much." She hesitated as she looked at her mother. "You seem to be doing well. I thought this was going to be a long road back for you."

"It's not as bad as it could have been," her mother said.

A shadow appeared in Wendy's eyes. "It is."

Her mother hesitated, struggling with concern.

"It will be all right, you'll see."

When Wendy said nothing, she continued, "I have four other daughters who don't need their mother wallowing in sorrow. Someday we'll be able to talk about it but not yet. But it really is OK."

"Wow..." Wendy said, looking down as she shook her head dismissively.

*   *   *

~ 2 ~

Revelation

Wendy was lying in bed, staring up at a ceiling that was not visible in the soft light filtering into the room through the sheer curtains. She turned onto her side and gazed at the crescent moon. She was thinking about Dolly.

She sat up, put her feet on the floor, and reached for the blue jeans on the chair beside the desk. A minute later, she stood, fully dressed beside the bed. She quietly slipped down the stairs and onto the porch.

This was Jenny's domain— the porch swing after dark. She often heard her mother find fault with her sister for her affection for the night.

She understood. *There is a magic to the night, especially a night such as this. Wow, I even sound like Jenny.*

A little bit, Dolly said.

Wendy was shocked, pleased, startled, and amazed to find the girl standing beside the swing.

"How did you..." Wendy's thoughts trailed off, as did her words.

I was out and about and saw you sitting here, Dolly said.

"You go out at night by yourself?"

Dolly nodded. *I thought you might like some company.*

"I do!" Wendy insisted. "But it's one o'clock in the morning!"

Dolly simply shrugged her shoulders. *Can we...* Dolly turned toward the street in front of the house as she spoke.

"*Can we what?*" Wendy asked.

Can we walk?

Wendy looked around before she answered. "I guess so..."

Come!

"I think you're leading me into mischief."

Probably, Dolly said. *Come.*

"I'm mystified and excited," Wendy said. "I've not done this; I've never sneaked out of my house to wander in the night. But I'm quite sure you have."

Oh yes.

"With my sister."

Dolly nodded.

"How do you do that?" Wendy asked.

Do what?

"How do you make the light shine through your dress?"

Did you notice... Dolly said. *I don't speak aloud?*

"What?" Wendy sputtered in surprise. "But I hear you! You don't..."

Dolly gazed into Wendy's eyes, saying nothing.

"I hear you in my head! Or in my mind, or something... how do you do that?"

Dolly nodded. *I haven't spoken aloud tonight, yet you hear me.*

"And that streetlight is shining right through you like you're a ghost!"

I can change it, Dolly said as her appearance grew

more solid, *but it is so much easier like this, especially when you're with friends.*

"What are you, Dolly?" Wendy asked, wide-eyed. "Please..."

What am I, Wendy?

"I think..." she hesitated. "I think you're a ghost. But I also think I'm quite asleep and I'm dreaming, so it's quite all right."

You were thinking of me?

Wendy's eyes flared with surprise in the moonlight.

"Yes," she said. "I slept briefly but awakened and simply lay in my bed, thinking."

Of me, Dolly said. *So, I came.*

"How did you know?"

Dolly shrugged her shoulders. *Are you sleeping? Are you dreaming?*

Wendy said nothing but gazed off into the night. "No. This is all too real. Everything but you."

I feel real, Dolly said.

Wendy simply gazed at her. After a few moments, she spoke.

"A real ghost?" Wendy mumbled.

I would hate to be any other kind, Dolly said, smiling.

"But you're not spooky, you're not"

Like a storybook ghost?

"Yeah..."

I'm just me, being who I am, I guess.

"How long have you been a ghost?" Wendy cautiously inquired.

Oh, maybe two hundred and fifty years...

"Then how were you able to be with Jenny?"

As I am with you.

"I would be terrified if I didn't want to be your friend so very much."

Am I scary? Dolly asked.

"No, no..." Wendy said. "I'm feeling a million things... but now I'm afraid that this is a dream and I shall awaken tomorrow, severely disappointed."

I will be near, Dolly said.

*   *   *

The next afternoon, Wendy struggled, hesitant to confront her mother. But the afternoon morphed into evening into the business of helping her mother with her younger sisters and setting the table for supper. Two hours later, the twins had gone to bed and Dawn was in her room doing homework.

Wendy approached her mother. "You knew," she said, trying to avoid sounding accusative but failing badly.

"What's that?" her mother asked.

Wendy steadied herself and spoke again. "You knew."

"Knew what? You're not making sense."

"About Dolly."

"Oh... that." She shrugged her shoulders dismissively. "Yes."

"I still can't even say it out loud; I've been wondering if the whole thing was a dream. The girl is a ghost who... I don't even know what to think about this... how..."

"I'm sure you'll work it out," her mother said. "The last two or three years of Jenny's life, she and Dolly were inseparable. But she is a ghost. That's why you never met her."

"That's beyond weird," Wendy said, "but it explains why Jenny never had any really close friends I mean, she did, but..."

"Yes," her mother said. "It took me quite a bit and it never really sinks in. Over time, you somehow accept it. You'll find that it is very easy to love that girl."

"So, you and Dolly..."

Janice nodded her head. "She's like another daughter to me."

"Why didn't we know?"

"She's invisible unless she wants you to see her."

"Where does she live? Where does she stay?" Wendy asked.

"There," her mother said, pointing to the alcove.

"Here?" Wendy asked. "In the house?"

"Yes. That's why her picture is on the wall," her mother said. "Dolly!"

Dolly appeared beside Wendy. In spite of her adventures the night before, Wendy startled and gasped at her sudden appearance.

"This is too much, too fast," Wendy said. "And you live here?"

"Yes. She watches over us," her mother said. "You and I and your sisters."

She turned to Dolly. "That's why you were at my school when I was walking home."

Dolly nodded.

"You're always around..."

No, I go a lot of places. But if there is a problem, I can be here immediately. I've been watching you since you were ten.

"That's when you first met Jenny. This keeps getting weirder and weirder," Wendy said.

Well, I was with a friend at the drive-in theater... Dolly said.

"A ghost friend?" Wendy asked.

Sure. My best friend is also a ghost, Dolly said, smiling sweetly as she vanished.

"A friend... a drive-in theater..." Wendy mumbled.

"Yeah," her mother said with a slight giggle. "She gets in free..."

"When we were walking home the other day," Wendy said, "three boys were bothering me and she scared one of them so badly she made him wet his pants! Really, he actually wet himself."

"Yeah, Dolly is no one to mess with. Very powerful, even for a ghost. She can get inside someone's head and cause them instant terror."

"That's what she did the other night?" Wendy asked.

"From what you're describing, yes," her mother said. "And I'll bet she was very unconcerned when she walked you home. She was watching over you."

"Like a guardian angel..." Wendy said softly. "Why didn't Jenny tell us about her?"

"Well, she told me. But we thought it was best that you

girls reach a certain maturity before we let you know. If any of you couldn't keep this quiet, it could cause quite a few problems for us."

"Yeah, I guess so..." she said.

*　　　*　　　*

Over the next week, Dolly was around every day. And Wendy had a million questions. Dolly helped her with her homework, or they would sit and chat. Dolly managed to kindle the same interest in history that Jenny had. She loved to listen to Dolly's firsthand accounts of things that happened long ago.

"Dolly knows so much about history," Wendy said to her mother one evening.

"Yes. She's lived it at least the last two hundred plus years," her mother replied. "And she is the most inquisitive girl I have ever met. Since the late seventeen hundreds she has followed everything that was going on. If there was a battle, she'd be there watching. She has witnessed, as far as I can determine, over a hundred battles, the sinking of a dozen ships, hundreds of fires, and the assassination of two presidents and that's only the start of the list. She doesn't want to miss out on anything."

"Yes!" Wendy said. "She told me about the opening of the Panama Canal and the construction of the Empire State Building."

"I went through a similar thing when I first met the girl," her mother said. "I had a million questions."

"How did you get to know her? Did you know she

was a ghost?"

"No. After Jenny got out of the hospital, she was talking quite a bit about her friend Dolly, who was a ghost; it concerned me quite a bit. I wanted to believe her, but I couldn't. I was beginning to think she was delusional, the result of the concussion she received in the accident. But Dolly wasn't having it. She wanted to meet me and get to know me. She was getting frustrated and impatient, so she came to the house and rang the front doorbell."

"She what?"

"She did," said her mother.

"A ghost rang your front doorbell? It sounds like a Halloween prank."

"She introduced herself as Dolly, but I still didn't believe her. I thought it was a practical joke. She had to disappear and reappear twice before I believed her."

"Wow..." Wendy said softly.

* * *

Another Star Wars movie? Jenny asked.

Yes, Dolly said. *They never stop; but they're pretty good.*

They were in a large tree at the entrance to the drive-in movie theater. The sun had set and the dusk was settling in around them.

There used to be a lot of drive-ins, Dolly said wistfully. *That was fifty years ago. Every town had one, some had two. You could choose what movie you wanted to see. There were so many of them around. Now, I think there are only two drive-ins in all of Massachusetts.*

What happened? Jenny asked.

I don't know. Maybe TV changed everything. But teenagers had so much fun at the drive-in! They would go cruising in their automobiles down to the carhop restaurant where they would meet their friends. And then they would go to the drive-in; the really cool guys had Convertibles. I used to love watching them.

Carhops? Jenny asked. *What's a carhop?*

Well, the carhops were waitresses on roller skates in hamburger fast food restaurants where you eat in your car. The customers would order food on the intercom and girls on roller skates would bring them their food on trays that would set on the window when it was lowered.

What's an intercom? Jenny asked.

It's what they used to call the speakers that we have in drive-through restaurants today, but they had one at every parking space. The car hops would bring your food out.

Oh, yeah, said Jenny. *That makes sense. What happens if they close all of the drive-in theaters?*

We can go to movie theaters but it's not as nice, or as much fun. I love being outdoors. The screen is huge and there is so much space.

Their conversation ended as the screen lit up and music started.

*   *   *

"What happened the other night?" Adam asked.

"Well...," Wendy hesitated. She didn't want to get Adam

worried. "I just missed the school bus."

"How did you get home?"

"I walked home,"

"Is that safe?"

"Yeah, I was with another girl, an older girl."

They were at the shooting range. When Adam and Janice started dating, he discovered Wendy's interest in guns and encouraged her to learn to shoot and it had become one of her favorite activities. She loaded her gun and slipped on ear protection as she waited for the target to set in place.

"How old is she?" he asked.

"What?" she asked as she slipped the ear protection off her ears.

"How old is she?"

"Fourteen or fifteen. She was a friend of Jenny's. I'm safe with her."

She saw the change in his eyes when she mentioned Jenny. *I should avoid mentioning her name,but I can't. I'm not going to forget her. He's going to have to man up and come to terms with it; if I can, he can.*

When Adam started dating her mother, Wendy thought that it was doomed because he was acting out of guilt. He was there when Jenny died and still carried the burden. But she soon realized that was not the case. He really liked her mother and they were quite natural together. And he loved the girls.

"Was your mother OK with that?" he asked.

"Yeah, we got hassled by some gang members but Dolly

scared them off."

"What?" he asked.

"Yeah, that's her name, Dolly. She's not afraid of anyone. Mom says she can be the scariest person she's ever met."

"How is she scary?" he asked.

"I don't know; she's just unafraid... and courageous. I think guys like that are just cowards and she seems to know that and she makes them afraid of *her* instead of the other way around."

"Does she go to your school?"

"No, I don't know where she goes. Maybe she's homeschooled."

She slipped her ear protection on, raised her gun and started shooting.

*   *   *

That's nice, Jenny said.

Dolly and Jenny were in their alcove watching. Their family was sitting at the dining table eating supper. Adam had been around a lot lately.

Oh? Dolly said.

Yeah, I like this. I like him a lot and I'm glad he's with mom. The girls really like him. He's taught Wendy to shoot and he took over her martial arts training. She was already one of the top athletes in the school and under Adam, she's become quite formidable.

And he's huge, Dolly said.

Yes, but he's a puppy dog, laughed Jenny.

*   *   *

~ 3 ~

Reunion

"I have a question," Wendy said.

She was sitting on the couch in the living room. Her mother was sitting in a stuffed chair across from her.

"How come..." Wendy hesitated. "Dolly? Are you around?"

She slowly glanced around the room. After a moment, the ghost appeared on the couch beside her.

"Is your question for Dolly and me?" her mother asked.

"Well, yeah... How come Dolly's here? I mean, Dolly's a ghost, and she's here with us." She turned to Dolly. "You died a long time ago and became a ghost."

Yes... Dolly answered slowly, encouraging Wendy to continue.

Wendy studied them both and then spoke. "Where's Jenny?"

The question caught them both off guard.

"She died..." Wendy said, grief creeping into her eyes. "Why isn't she here? Why isn't she a ghost? Why can't she be here? This doesn't make sense! If you're here, then why isn't she? I thought you were her best friend!"

"Ah..." Janice said carefully. "She is a ghost."

"Then why isn't she here!!!" Wendy demanded. "Why doesn't she come around?"

She is... Dolly said carefully.

Wendy was shifting from grief to anger. "Then why can't I see her?" she demanded as she burst into tears. "This isn't fair! Do I mean that little to her?"

"You mean a lot to her!" Janice exclaimed. "She loves you very much."

"Jenny and your mother and I talked about this," Dolly said. "She wants very much to see you, but we didn't want to do this too much, too fast. There are no self-help books out on how to introduce your children to their ghost siblings."

"Yes," her mother interjected. "We decided to have you meet Dolly, and after you got used to the idea, we could have you see Jenny again. We thought it would be too much for you to meet Dolly and your ghost sister all at once."

"When can I see her?" she demanded.

*　　*　　*

Jenny was there when Dolly and Wendy first met; she was there when Wendy realized that Dolly was a ghost; she had watched their friendship grow. It was Jenny who insisted that Wendy first get used to the idea that Dolly was a ghost before they re-introduced her to Jenny. She had waited some time for the moment when Wendy would ask the question. And that had just happened.

Janice looked around the room and called out. "Jenny?"

She would never forget the look on her younger sister's face when she slowly materialized in front of her.

Wendy's world stopped. It was her dead sister that stood right in front of her.

"Jenny?" she mumbled through tears. "That's really you?"

Yes, Jenny said.

Wendy turned to her mother. "I can't. I don't..."

Her mother knelt in front of her and took both her hands. "Yes, this is your sister. She's a ghost, just like Dolly. They hang around together like best friends do. Whenever Dolly isn't here, she's been with Jenny. She is still with us still a member of the family."

She looked up at her mother, then at Jenny.

"I'm going to leave you two alone," her mother said. She stood, turned, and walked out of the living room as Dolly disappeared.

"I missed you so badly!" Wendy wailed, tears crawling down her face. "I want to hug you so badly, but you're not real. No, I don't mean you're not real, I mean I just I can't believe you're here. I never—when you died, I was so sad! I didn't think I'd ever see you again."

Shhh, Jenny said.

The next moment, Wendy felt lifted as her sister surrounded her with affection. The sadness vanished, her tears were gone, and the pain in her chest no longer there. The tears that remained were of joy, and she was blessed with a happiness she had never known.

* * *

Janice stood, looking through the kitchen window, watching Dawn as she left the house. At the bottom of the driveway, a girl with dark green hair, heavy black lipstick, and a nose ring waited for her.

Who is that? Jenny asked as she appeared beside Janice.

That is Henge, Dawn's new best friend.

What's her real name? Jenny asked. *No one would name their kid that.*

Stonehenge.

Of course, Jenny said as the two girls disappeared around the corner. *She's a freak; I'm sure her parents are bigger freaks.*

I know, Janice said, frustrated. *And...?*

I don't know; just an observation.

Do you think she's trouble? Janice asked.

I don't know... Jenny *said. I can find out anything and everything about her if you want...*

No, I need to trust her. They've done nothing to even arouse my suspicion.

The girl looks like trouble, said Jenny.

I get it, Janice said, turning away from the window, heading toward the living room.

*   *   *

"Are you going to marry him?" Wendy asked.

Her mother turned to look at her but said nothing. After a moment, she spoke.

"I think he's getting ready to ask me," she said quietly.

"And?"

"This is a huge decision."

"Do you love him?" Wendy asked.

Janice stared out the window for a moment, then answered. "Very much so."

"It's a problem," Wendy said.

"How?"

"Jenny and Dolly," Wendy answered. "You will have to tell him."

"Yes," her mother said. "I guess I will."

"And?"

"And what?" Janice asked.

"Not everyone is as open to this as you and I. He's a soldier and a cop. How open do you think he would be to this? He might freak out."

"Well, he would have to accept it. They are my daughters. If he can't deal with it, then I can't marry him."

"How would you do that?" Wendy asked. "Are you going to wait until he asks before you lower the boom?"

"That's a good question," her mother said.

Wendy stared off for a moment then spoke. "I think I can handle this, I've got an idea; yes, I've got this."

*   *   *

"Are you ready to go?" Adam asked.

She was sitting with three of her girlfriends on the polished floor of the Dojo. Adam had been bringing Wendy to Karate class regularly and had become close friends with the sensei. The students eagerly looked forward to sparring demonstrations between the two masters.

"Yeah," she said as she got to her feet. She turned back to one of the girls. "Julie, do you need a ride?"

"My mom's coming, I'm fine."

As they headed to the truck, Adam started making small talk.

"Another six months and you'll be ready for your black belt."

"I need more weight training," she said. "I need to develop more upper body strength. I don't want to compete against girls only."

"You get that in your training for the girl's gymnastics, don't you?"

"Yeah, it just takes time," she said.

"True, that," Adam said as he pulled the truck onto the highway.

"I have a question," Wendy said. "And you have to give me a straight answer; no avoiding the question."

"You sound so bossy."

"There's a good reason for that," she said.

"What is that?" she said.

"I *am* bossy."

"That explains everything," he said.

She shrugged her shoulders. After a moment she spoke. "A deal?"

"Well, yeah. Unless it's something I shouldn't talk about."

"OK... You could take the sensei in a full contact match, couldn't you? You hold back, I know you do. I think you're a very powerful fighter."

He thought for a moment before he spoke. "Um... Yeah, I think I could."

"But, you don't..."

"Yeah, well... It would be bad... um, etiquette, bad business. You don't defeat a guy in his own house, in front of his own students. That would be beyond rude."

"As long as we're being open and honest," he continued, "I want to ask you something; tell me about your ghosts. Do you see them regularly? How did you get to meet them?"

"Our house is haunted," she said unemotionally.

"What?" he asked.

"Yeah, there are two ghosts in our house. I talk to them all the time. Well, I don't *talk* to them... it's kind of hard to explain but we sort of communicate."

"Really? I think you just have a very big imagination," he said.

"I thought you were *interested* in my ghosts," she said.

"I am. But you say you talk to ghosts, or "communicate" with them. I think that you're imagining it. You're making up imaginary friends. A lot of kids do that."

"Well," she said, shrugging her shoulders. "I guess mom imagines them as well; she sees them and "communicates" with them."

"What? Your mother? You know I'm going to go ask her."

"Feel free," she said.

"Wow, so, you're not just putting me on..."

"No, I'm not."

*   *   *

~ 4 ~

An Introduction and a Reunion

"Who's the extra place for?" Adam asked.

The twins were setting the table as Adam grabbed a beer from the refrigerator. He twisted the top off, opened the cabinet under the sink, and dropped the cap into the trash.

"A friend of Wendy's," Janice said.

"Do I know her?"

"She's that girl I told you about who walked me home when I missed the bus," Wendy said.

"Yeah, what's her name... Dolly?"

"Yeah," Wendy said.

One of the twins sat down across from Adam.

"Which one are you?" he asked.

"I'm Debbie; she's Lizzie."

"Do you have a middle name?"

"Yes, Elaine."

"What's her middle name?"

"Elaine."

"Wait a minute, you're Deborah Elaine Jeffries," Adam said to Debbie, "and she's Elizabeth Elaine Jeffries? How do you both have the same middle name?"

"It was a mix-up in the birth certificates," Janice said. "Lizzie was supposed to be named Elizabeth Jean, but both certificates had the same middle name."

"Couldn't you get them changed?" Adam asked.

"I suppose..." Janice said, "but there was red tape and we procrastinated, which made the red tape more extensive. Then the doctor who signed the birth certificates died, which made it even more complicated. And suddenly the twins were four, and they wouldn't let us make the change, which was a relief."

"They wouldn't let you..."

"We decided it was acceptable," Lizzie said.

"We like having the same middle name," Debbie said. "I don't think there will be any confusion between us; everyone calls us by our first names."

"Okay..." Adam said doubtfully.

"It takes a while," Janice said, "but you'll get there. One day one of them will walk into the room and you will immediately know who it is."

"Unless, of course," Wendy glanced at one and then the other, "they don't want you to."

"That's true," Janice replied. "They play the twin switch game all the time; I'm the only one they can't fool."

Debbie shrugged her shoulders.

*   *   *

Fifteen minutes later Dolly arrived, and they all sat down for supper. Dolly was dressed in blue jeans and a silver sweater with a green print design, and really nice shoes.

"Where did you get that sweater? I am so jealous!" Wendy exclaimed.

At the mall; there's a new place there that has the nic-

est stuff; I forget the name. I'll show you next time we go.

Conversation diminished as the supper was served, but resumed when the meal was finished.

"So, Dolly," Adam asked, "how did you and Wendy meet?"

Well, I was Jenny's best friend. I had seen Wendy around but never really knew her. Then I saw those boys bothering her the other night, so I intervened, and we've been really good friends ever since.

"How did you scare those boys off?"

Well... I have my ways..., she said mysteriously.

"Do you fight? Wendy and I train at the dojo. Wendy's getting really good."

I don't fight; I don't have to. I just know how to handle people and situations.

"That's mysterious; you're mysterious," he said with a look of doubt.

"She has her ways," Janice interjected.

"Where do you go to school? Did you meet Jenny at school?"

I'm homeschooled, she said nonchalantly.

"Where did you meet Jenny?"

At the graveyard, she said with a straight face.

"At the what?" he said.

"Okay, why don't we head into the living room," Janice said. "Girls, can you take care of everything?"

"You girls clear the table," Dawn said to the twins. "I'll put the food away and set up the dishwasher."

"Okay," one of the girls said as they started

grabbing dishes.

"Let's go in the living room and talk," Janice said. "Adam, I'm going to have some wine. Do you want some?"

"No, I'll just grab another beer."

*　　*　　*

Wendy sat beside Dolly on the short couch; Adam and Janice sat across from them on the bigger sectional couch. The twins were in their rooms doing homework; Dawn was in the TV room watching her favorite doctor show.

"So, are you going to continue going to Thayer?" Adam asked Wendy. "There are some nice private schools around."

"Yeah, it has a good bit of Jenny about it; she liked it, I like it."

"Yeah...," Adam said grimly.

"Don't be like that!" Wendy scolded.

"Well, I..." he stuttered uncomfortably.

"If I can get over it, you can get over it," Wendy said.

Wow, Janice thought, *she doesn't cut him any slack.*

She doesn't cut anyone any slack, Dolly said.

They talked about Thayer as Adam attempted to get Dolly to discuss homeschooling, but she just shrugged her shoulders.

I know history better than anyone, she said.

Wendy turned to her mother. "I told Adam our house was haunted and about the two ghosts, but he doesn't believe me."

Adam glanced toward Janice to see her reaction.

"She knows all about it," Wendy said. "One of them,

I talk to all the time. Their favorite thing is the drive-in movie theater."

"So," Adam said, "you have two ghosts in this house. And you "communicate" with them."

"Yes," Janice said emphatically.

"That is out there, a bit much for me," Adam said.

"What? A big bruiser like you is afraid of ghosts?" Wendy said teasingly.

"No..." he growled.

"You could meet them..." Janice said.

"Oh, I'm sure," Adam said sarcastically.

"If you're up to it..." Wendy teased.

"I wouldn't have any trouble with that if I actually believed it."

I don't think he's up to it! Dolly said, joining in the teasing.

"Okay, I'll call your bluff! Bring on your ghosts!" he said.

"Dolly can help you with that," Janice said.

"How?" he asked.

The three females looked at each other conspiratorially. Then Janice looked at Adam and tilted her head toward Dolly. Adam looked at Dolly and then at Wendy, who nodded her head toward Dolly.

"What? Dolly?" he asked confusedly.

Yes, Adam. I'm a ghost. I was born in Shawmut in 1760.

"You look remarkable for someone who died two hundred and fifty years ago. And what is Shawmut? Is it in New England? Is it in America? I think it's in never-neverland."

Today, they call it Boston, Dolly said.

"Boston used to be called Shawmut?" he asked.

Well, the name changed before I was born, but a lot of people stubbornly hung on to the name, so technically I was born in Boston.

"You're avoiding the subject," Wendy said. "How do you know Dolly isn't a ghost? Can you prove it?"

"I think I'm having the biggest practical joke in history being pulled on me right now. Okay, you guys got me! You almost had me believing! And the three of you are in it together. This is masterful! And Wendy started on me a few days ago; it was genius, and I got pulled right in. Every time I start thinking I'm the sharpest bend in the road, something like this comes along and puts me in my place. I think you need to prove that Dolly is a ghost."

"Adam " Janice started.

I've got this, mom, Dolly said.

"Mom? She's your daughter?" Adam sputtered.

Adam! You don't believe in me? Dolly said.

"Well, of course I believe in you! You're right in front of me."

Give me your hand, Dolly said as she reached her arm across to him.

He gave her a cautious look and carefully extended his hand toward hers.

"What the hell?" he said as he scrambled back in his chair and quickly stood. "Her hand isn't there! My hand went right through hers!"

You don't believe in me, Dolly said teasingly.

"I don't know what to believe!"

We'll try this then...

As she stared into his eyes, she started to slowly fade.

"What the—she's... Is she coming back?"

I'm here, she said.

Adam turned toward her voice and found her standing behind him in a long, flowing dress.

*   *   *

Janice had one glass of wine; Adam finished the bottle and was a bit tipsy. Dolly had to disappear and reappear several times before Adam finally settled down.

" What's your full name?" Adam inquired.

Dolores Erin Clahane.

"That name—the grave beside Jenny's..."

Yes, she said proudly. *I am that ghost. Janice cleaned up my gravesite and got me a new stone identical to Jenny's. She's my adopted mother; this is my family.*

Adam turned to Janice before he spoke.

"You adopted a ghost?"

"Well, we didn't sign any papers or anything like that, but—"

"You were at the supper table, eating with us," he said to Dolly. "How did you do that?"

An illusion. when I do it really well, it seems like I'm eating.

"Wow..." Adam said. "You understand if it takes me a bit to get used to this."

Well, when we met, you talked with me for an hour, and you didn't suspect a thing? Do you notice that I am not speaking out loud?

"What? Say that again."

I'm not speaking aloud.

"But you're moving your lips..."

Sometimes I do that..., she said, shrugging her shoulders.

"Now I get it!" he said.

What? Dolly asked.

"How you met Jenny!"

"What?" Janice asked.

"Yes," Wendy said. "In the graveyard."

"Jenny had about a dozen ghost friends in the grave-yard; she was a natural medium," Janice said. "Wait until you meet Malcolm..."

Do you remember when Jenny was in the hospital in a coma? Dolly asked.

"That was before Jenny and Adam met," Janice said. "They met that fall after Jenny came out of the coma. She started school at Thayer that fall."

Oh yes, that's right, said the ghost.

"You said there were two ghosts that were haunting your house," Adam said. "Where is the other one?"

The other one is Jenny, Dolly said.

Adam got a shocked look on his face. He sat frozen, just staring at Janice and the two girls.

"No..., Oh my god!" he exclaimed. His mouth sagged open.

Janice snuggled in against Adam. "Would you like to see her again?" she asked.

"Don't play with me..." he looked at her with startled,

pleading eyes.

"Hey, they made me wait two weeks after I met Dolly before they told me about Jenny!" Wendy said, "and it was like pulling teeth!"

Adam was still staring into Janice's face.

"Yeah," Janice said softly. "She's here."

Dolly gestured to the stuffed chair that sat at a right angle to the couches. Slowly she took form. She was wearing the outfit that she died in, yet it was unmarred.

"Hi," she said cautiously.

Adam sat, stunned, saying nothing. Slowly his eyes started getting heavy with moisture, but he was still silent.

It is so good to see you, my old friend, she said softly. *I've been watching you and waiting for so long to talk with you again.*

"My god," he mumbled. Grief was welling in his eyes as he slid off the couch into a kneeling position in front of her chair. He started to reach out and take her hand in his but realized that wasn't possible.

"I can hardly believe what I'm seeing. Could you..."

What? asked Jenny.

"Could you change?" he asked.

Into what? she asked confusedly.

"That outfit..."

It was as if a wave passed over her, and she was sitting wearing a long, multi-pastel angel-type dress.

"Yes," Adam said, "you don't go to the mall with Wendy and Dolly?"

Sometimes, but Dolly likes colloquial dress; I prefer

traditional.

"Traditional?"

For angels and some ghosts, Jenny said.

"Angels?" Adam asked.

I'm kidding, Jenny said.

Adam stared at her for a moment before he spoke.

"Aren't you supposed to...move on..., or something?"

She briefly looked puzzled. *You mean to wherever? Not that I've seen... No one has told us anything.*

I guess we could, Dolly interjected, *but we're fine here.*

I'm so glad you're seeing my mother, Jenny said. *Are you going to ask her to marry you?*

He sat speechless as he sat in his kneeling position in front of the ghost of the girl he had seen gunned down.

*   *   *

~ 5 ~

Demon

The early morning fog was dissipating before the morning sun, creating a light reflection off the sea of tree-top leaves in the forest below them.

Springtide has always been my favorite time to be a ghost, Dolly said. *Especially in New England. In about forty days it goes from a frozen land beneath ice and snow to a land that is green and alive and everything is blossoming; everything is new and fresh. I don't know what I love the most—all of the blossoming flowers or the dark, beautiful rivers that flow so swiftly.*

Springtide? Jenny asked.

Yes. What do you...? Oh! You say springtime; that's incorrect. It is just people being lazy with English words. The word is 'springtide.' The time from the vernal equinox to the summer solstice.

The what? Jenny asked.

The vernal equinox. You know... Dolly insisted.

I don't, Jenny said.

Vernal means spring, and the equinox is a day when the day and the night are exactly the same length. It only happens twice a year, around the 20th of March and the 22nd of September. So, the vernal equinox is the one that happens in the spring. In September, you have the au-

tumn equinox. *The summer solstice is the longest day of the year, and the winter solstice is the shortest. Solstice comes from a word that means 'the sun stopped.' Superstition was that the sun actually stopped on that day, but it didn't really.*

That's a good thing, Jenny said. *When did you learn all this?*

In the third grade.

You learned that in the third grade? Jenny seemed surprised.

Yes, I told you, we graduated from school in the sixth grade. And we were well educated.

Wow, I was born in the wrong time period... Jenny said grimly.

Dolly shrugged her shoulders. *We looked at the sky all the time. Your sky is drowned out by the city lights. We traveled by the stars, and we always knew where we were.*

Nothing was said as the two ghosts returned their attention to the day around them.

My favorite thing is trees, Jenny said. *Trees are so amazing. Not all trees, but there are a lot of trees that are incredible. There are huge trees that are hundreds of years old with massive branches, and there are trees that are beautiful with lacy leaves that just sway in the wind. Sometimes I get into the top of a big, beautiful tree, and I permeate the crown and I just sway. The wind...*

Yes, I know some truly amazing trees.

Yes! Jenny replied. *You can learn history from them. And they're so alive. And you can get to know them so well.*

Yes, Dolly said. *I had forgotten that. I'm getting old. I was quite interested in trees for a while, but after World War II, there was a lot of building and construction of big highways, and it was a big distraction. There is one tree that I used to frequent in Brookline Village that was quite nice. But I haven't been there for, probably, sixty years. I'll have to go find it sometime soon. I remember that tree on Boston Harbor below the hospital; you used to hide in it.*

Yeah... Jenny said dreamily. *You know, when you permeate a flock of birds or a school of fish, sometimes it feels like they're indifferent. You're there, and they can't do anything about it. I'm getting better with this, but still... But anyway, with trees, it's... I can't describe it. It's like I love them so much, and they love me. We're just being there, being the same thing. And I love how I think when I'm being a tree. My memory suddenly goes back a hundred years. Their long, long memory becomes my memory. I can remember when I was a small sapling and the New England countryside was so full of trees.*

And children! she continued. *I was being this big old oak tree one time, and I scanned back through the years, looking at the hundreds of children who have climbed my branches. Children love trees. And the trees love the children.*

And your space is different when you're being a tree. They never move! So, if a tree is two hundred years old, its whole life is all about that grove they stand in. I love their serenity and contemplation.

*   *   *

Adam, Jenny, and Dolly were sitting at the picnic table under the big tree behind the school. It was late afternoon, and the sun was heading toward the horizon. Adam had a million questions. He had exhausted Jenny of answers and now was deep in a discussion with Dolly about the history of Boston.

"So, you weren't really homeschooled?" Adam asked.

Well, some. Most of my education was in a one-room schoolhouse. I graduated from the sixth grade in 1772, if I remember correctly.

"You didn't get much of an education," Adam remarked, "but you seem to be one of the most educated girls I know."

In the 1770s, a graduate of the sixth grade received a better education than a college student does today. I doubt that most of the college graduates could pass the exam I was given as a requirement to graduate from the sixth grade.

"Wow," Adam said. "I had no idea."

Why don't I introduce you to someone who knows the subject even better than myself? Dolly said.

"I find it hard to believe that person exists," he said.

He does; this school... Jenny said, *who was it named after?*

"Thaddeus P. Thayer," Adam said. "He was some famous guy back in the 1800s. I don't know what he did."

He was a well-known educator and author,

Jenny added.

"And?" Adam asked.

He's here, Dolly said. *Would you like to meet him?*

"What? Wow," Adam said. "Really?"

Do you have your keys to the school on you? Jenny asked.

"Yes..."

Let's go.

*   *   *

What was that?

I don't know, Dolly said. *You felt it, too?*

Jenny nodded. *What is it?*

I don't know, but it's dark...

Jenny followed Dolly into the turbulence of a developing storm in the night sky above their home. Time seemed to stop as she watched Dolly scan the graveyard with a bristling intensity that seemed to almost glow.

Rain started to fall as Jenny silently kept her attention fixed on Dolly.

Jenny had no problem letting Dolly take command of the situation; she had been a ghost about a year; Dolly had been one for two and a half centuries. Jenny couldn't imagine what types of afflictions and horrors Dolly had encountered.

At some point, lightning stabbed across the sky above them. A moment later, thunder fractured the atmosphere, as Dolly gasped.

What! Jenny demanded.

Come! Caution!

As she followed to the oldest section of the graveyard, Dolly was changing into something Jenny had never encountered in any ghost; intense emotion emanated from her, and she suddenly seemed ancient. It wasn't anger; it seemed to be a burning disgust and rejection of what, Jenny couldn't begin to guess.

Below them, in the far corner, were three or four mounds—burial crypts. Suddenly Dolly latched onto Jenny and pulled her into one of the tombs. Jenny found herself confronted with what would best be described as a most intense wickedness. It was a seething, reeking manifestation of evil beyond anything Jenny had ever imagined.

Hold me, Dolly commanded, *and anchor yourself!*

Jenny latched onto Dolly and permeated the mound surrounding them, anchoring them both.

In the blinding light of Dolly's flash, Jenny saw two people, living beings, screaming as they fled the tomb. Jenny was stunned with what Dolly had become; it was a fire that was not a flame; it was a spark of tenacious, burning emotion beyond a human realm.

Dolly's attack on the evil, semi-solid apparition was not a permeation but a powerful, high-impact overwhelm. With a soundless scream, the shade shattered into a violent scattering of filth and debris, of dark images and the gelatinous manifestation of suppression, darkness, and corruption.

She watched Dolly tear into the specter's memory, forcing the darkly wretched sequence of horrific incidents back into the black consciousness of the dark wraith. With a shattering cacophony of noise and sensation, a soul-crippling scream burst across the sky.

Then, stillness.

*   *   *

Go help your sister, Dawn, Dolly said, *don't hesitate to reveal yourself.*

Jenny looked down on her sister; curled into a fetal position, she resembled a corpse that had succumbed to intense terror. Jenny realized that Dawn was one of the two figures she saw fleeing the crypt. The girl opened her eyes and stared up at Jenny.

Hi... Are you OK?

"Did you come back to save me?" Dawn pleaded, trembling. "Am I dead?"

You're alive. Tell me about it.

"Henge..."

Jenny waited for the girl's trembling to cease or at least lessen to the point where she could speak.

Over the next twenty minutes, Jenny listened to a story of two teenage girls dabbling into the occult with its symbols, tomes, and tokens to a point of sufficient success to attract the attention of a fairly powerful entity. What they had attracted, Dolly may know, but Jenny did not.

She listened for two hours, getting the girl to go over the story a sufficient number of times to release its grip on her.

Then she permeated the girl, driving away any hint or memory of evil and supplanting it with her love, to the point where the girl spoke calmly and rationally.

"You came back to save me?"

I never went away, said Jenny. *I have been watching over the family since my departure.*

"I'm, I don't know..."

There is a lot to discuss. I shall be around; we will talk. You should sleep; when you awaken, find your mother. I must be off.

Ten minutes later, Dawn was sleeping soundly.

*   *   *

The sound of the dishwasher intruded slightly into the living room as Janice settled into the recliner; supper was over, and the twins were off to bed. Dawn had been ill in bed for two days. Janice was going to go to her room and check on her, but first she needed to relax with a cup of coffee.

Jenny and Dolly appeared.

We must talk, Jenny said.

Janice said nothing but waited for Jenny to speak.

Dawn... and Henge. They got themselves into a good bit of trouble.

With boys? Janice asked, *with school?*

With the occult, Dolly said.

The occult?

Yes. You've watched Henge get more involved with her goth jewelry, piercings, and tattoos. Dolly said, *And Dawn was following her.*

She wanted to get a tattoo and some piercings, but I forbid it, Janice said. *She got some sort of temporary tat-*

too, and I let her know I wasn't happy with it, but I didn't make her remove it. I was hoping it was a passing thing that would soon be gone.

Well, to make a long story short, Dolly said, *two days ago, in some ritual in one of the crypts in the far corner of the graveyard, they succeeded in attracting an evil of some substance. I don't know how; I don't know where they got the material; it's hard to acquire, but it seems that Henge was determined.*

What happened? Janice asked. *Is she in some sort of danger?*

No, Jenny said. *Dolly crushed it. Done, finished.*

That was when Dawn became ill, Janice speculated. *I knew something was going on but I failed to act. I really wanted her to make her own decisions...*

Yes, Jenny said, *but I've been spending some time with her, helping her get well.*

You revealed yourself...?

Yes, but I was not the first apparition to be revealed to her; she assumed that I had come back from the dead to save her. We've done a lot of talking; she'll be fine but she still thinks I'm some sort of angel. It took me over two hours to pull her from her terror. She was scared sense-less; I'm certain she will never go near the dark side again.

Wow... Janice mused, *I don't have any normal chil-dren. They're all...*

Exceptional... Dolly interjected.

Yeah, Janice agreed.

* * *

~ 6 ~

Dolly's Dilemma

Jennie sensed a change of mood in Dolly. She settled into the girl's space.

What? asked Dolly, responding to Jenny's attention.

What's happening? Jennie asked.

Just thinking.

Jennie said nothing, knowing she would continue. *She's struggling with something,* Jenny thought to herself. *What could be so serious that she would struggle with? She lives a very uncomplicated life.*

I think I want to go back, Dolly said.

Go back where? Jennie asked.

To life.

You have a life. What are you talking about?

After a brief hesitation, she spoke.

I think I want to be alive, she said cautiously.

You were alive; you died. End of story.

No, Dolly said, *I can be alive.*

Alive... You mean... What? I'm confused, Jennie said.

You know when you're in the womb and you get born as a baby and you have a mother and a father and you go to school and grow up to be an adult?

Now I'm even more confused. You already did that. You lived your life and you died. You never got to be an

222

adult, but you did that.

I think I want to go back.

What? How?

Just go back. I've seen ghosts do it. Actually, most ghosts do it; that's why our neighborhood isn't overrun with a billion ghosts.

You mean like reincarnation? Jenny asked.

Well, I don't want to come back as a flower or a bee-tle, but yes.

That's a myth! Jennie *said. That's not true!*

You mean like ghosts? Dolly replied. *Ghosts are a myth; just ask anyone...*

What? Jenny said. *Ghosts come back in another life?*

Yes. I think most people have lived before, Dolly said. *Many times.*

Why don't they know that? Why don't they remember?

I don't know... Dolly said wistfully. *Maybe it's best if they don't remember. I mean, what if they were a bad person? Maybe they just need a fresh start without bad memories. I don't really know. But a ghost can go back.*

How—what... Jenny stuttered.

How do they what? asked Dolly.

Go back... Jenny said.

I don't know! Dolly snapped. *I can tell you anything about being a ghost, but not about this! I think maybe you find a pregnant woman...*

You— Jenny was struggling with her words. *You are the most certain person I've ever known. You have no un-certainties. If you don't totally know something, you just shrug your shoulders and don't bother. But with this, you are struggling; you're uncertain. I've never seen this.*

Dolly gave Jenny an apprehensive look.

You're afraid... Jenny said. *Why would you do this if you're not sure?*

Yes, I'm scared! Dolly said with a determined look, *but I need to do this.*

Why? Why would you want to do this? Jenny asked.

I want to feel things with my fingertips. I want to run my fingers through my beautiful head of hair. I want to feel my bare feet standing in a puddle and rain on my head. I want to feel the wind, I want to feel wet or hot or tired. I want to meet boys and flirt with them. I want to have babies someday!

Wow, Jenny said softly, *I never...*

I don't know... Dolly said frustratedly.

Jenny felt a sudden stab of loss.

What about me? Jenny demanded. *What do I do? I mean, you just leave? You just leave me here?*

Of course not! You were alive and we were together. You were alive and I was your best friend. If I'm alive, you can still be my best friend, the same way. Don't think about it now, Dolly said. *That's just what I've been thinking. It doesn't mean a thing.*

People can really do that? Go back and live more lives? Jenny asked.

I've seen it, Dolly said. *Many, many times.*

*   *   *

I don't understand, Jenny said.

What have you learned about being a ghost? Thaddeus asked.

I really believe we are people...,

Of course we are, Thaddeus interjected, *Ghosts are people, too. The difference between us and them, is that we don't have bodies; we are free of the flesh.*

Another thing I don't understand is the occult, Jenny said.

Because it's all rubbish! Thaddeus said, *Archaic methods of controlling people!*

Malcolm says that we are ghosts because we are made in the image of the creator, but I don't fully understand that.

Malcolm possesses great wisdom, Thaddeus said, *he's right.*

How is that?

Life is of the creator, and in that, life never dies.

What?

Life never dies; whether it is in the form of a person with a body or a ghost, life is immortal—flesh will pass but life will continue. That is the greatest gift of the creator; it created life and only the creator can end life.

Forever?

And always, Thaddeus said. *Think about life—rational thought would deliver you to the conclusion that life is cyclic* he continued, *it is born into flesh, lives, dies, and is born again.*

What about you and I? And Dolly?

I do believe we are procrastinators, Thaddeus said, *but then our creator also endowed us with power of choice.*

Dolly wants to go back.

Ah, Thaddeus said, *now I understand the guidance you seek.*

I am...

You're scared, confused and facing an impending loss. Jenny nodded.

There is no reason you should lose your connection; you can follow her as she grows; you can preserve and continue your friendship.

That's what she said, Jenny mused.

*   *   *

Jenny and Dolly looked down at two dozen people; probably nine children in the pool and a half dozen people seated at various tables between the pool and the house. On the huge lawn four boys were throwing a football. Closer to the house Adam's brother, Seth, was talking to another man while tending the barbeque. Wendy sat between Adam and his 17-year-old cousin, Randy, at one of the rented tables. Randy's best friend, Joseph, was sitting beside Dawn, unsuccessfully flirting. Janice was standing off to the side talking to Adam's mother, Helen.

"Dawn is my second oldest. She's a year younger than Wendy, who just turned fourteen. Wendy's a scrapper but

Dawn... she's still finding her way," Janice said wistfully. The twins will be nine soon, and they are rascals—in constant conspiracy to get into mischief, but never real trouble. You work with the twins; sometimes you negotiate. You don't try to outsmart them—They are such a handful!

"Well, I have Adam, and Seth you know. And you haven't met either of my daughters. Brenda is married with two kids. They live in Phoenix. Her sister Mara is away at college." She paused and looked over at the table where Adam and Wendy sat.

"What's going on with Wendy and my nephew?" Helen asked.

"It'll never happen," Randy said. "I get that you're training her but I think you're biased. I'm 20 pounds heavier and I'm quite sure I'm much faster."

"You're quite fast in the talking part," said Wendy. "But it didn't make much of an impact over here."

"Ooooh! burn!" chanted Joseph.

"What?" Randy stuttered his disbelief. "There's no way. You know that! It's not even worth discussing!"

"Discussing... oh you're still back in the talking part..." Wendy said nonchalantly.

"Randy..." Adam cautioned. "I wouldn't be so fast..."

Joseph leaned over to Randy and mumbled something about attitude—her attitude.

"Randy," Adam continued. "For the last three months I've been sparring full contact with this girl. She is scary..."

"I sensed that from the terror I'm feeling," Randy said

sarcastically.

"There's one way you can solve that terror," Wendy said, matching his sarcasm. "Out there on the lawn."

"You're kidding! You'd get your butt kicked. And I don't like picking on girls!"

"That's not what I've heard in school," Wendy said coyly.

"WHOA! Burn number 2!" Joseph chanted.

"Number three," Lizzie corrected. "Try to keep up!"

Adam turned to Wendy. "What are you doing?"

"I'm calling his bluff," she replied.

"You're challenging him to a fight?" Adam asked. *She's really pushing for this,* he thought. *I hope she knows what she's doing.*

"Well, some sparring..." she said as she shrugged her shoulders. "Nothing serious. Besides, I haven't beaten up any guys in at least a week. I'm due."

"Oh great! Here comes your mother!" said Randy.

"What's going on here?" she asked with a suspicious look in her eye.

"Wendy's going to kick Randy's butt!" exclaimed Lizzie. She and her twin sister, Debbie had surreptitiously inserted themselves into the conversation.

"What?" Janice said.

"I'm simply going to impart an education upon this individual..." Wendy said sarcastically.

"Wendy's going to kick his butt!" Debbie said.

"Adam?" she said, turning her attention toward him.

He held up his hands, pretending to have no part in the matter. "This is between these two."

"What's this about someone kicking someone's butt?"

"Wendy's going to kick Randy's butt", Lizzie repeated.

"It's nothing, mom. We just need to settle something with a little friendly combat," Wendy said.

"There is such a thing? What are you doing?" she demanded, turning toward Wendy.

"We're just settling a point. It's no big thing. The worse that could happen would be Randy getting a bloody nose. No big deal!"

She turned to Adam. "Are you...?"

"It wouldn't be that big a deal. They're not angry or upset at each other, there is just a little bit of an ego struggle here. I think it would be OK."

"You are as bad as she is!" Janice said to Adam. "I'm putting the responsibility of this on you! If anything happens..." She gave him a look of warning and turned away.

"So, you're serious, you want to settle this with combat?" Randy asked.

"it's a strong word," Wendy said, "but we don't want to leave this unsettled; if you want to be my boyfriend..."

"Who said anything about a boyfriend?"

She shrugged her shoulders. "It's a chance of a lifetime..." she said coyly.

"OK!" he said as he turned toward the lawn.

"Yes!" chanted Debbie and Lizzie in unison as they all got up to follow Randy.

What is going on down there? Dolly asked.

Our ninja-assassin sister just challenged Adam's cousin to combat.

You're kidding! Dolly said.

Yeah, the last couple of months she's become rather serious about this. I am glad she is not a cruel person because she is fierce; I wouldn't want to mess with her.

Wow, Dolly said. *The little girl I defended near the school in the spring has become a contender.*

I guess, said Jenny. *Not the same girl.*

*   *   *

There were a dozen people on the lawn surrounding the opponents. Dolly got Adam's attention and spread her hands to either side, as if asking 'what's this?'. Adam simply shrugged his shoulders.

Adam stepped in between the two. "OK, this is a friendly competition. No nastiness, no dirty fighting, no intention to hurt your opponent. You both get what I mean."

They both nodded their heads in agreement.

"What's the bet?" Lizzie asked.

"Yeah, what's the bet?" Debbie mimicking her twin sister.

"The loser gets pushed into the deep end of the pool, fully clothed!" Yelled Joseph.

"Agreed," said Randy.

"Yeah," Wendy said nodding.

Wendy calmly faced Randy, hands at her side. She turned to face him as he maneuvered around her.

Janice took Adam's hand into hers as the match started.

"Can she get hurt?" she asked.

"It's not her I'm worried about."

"Adam, would you explain this to me?" said a voice from behind them. They turned to see his mother, standing with her two best friends, Gertrude and Anna.

"Well, you know I've been training Wendy in martial arts? Well, they're just putting on a friendly demonstration."

"Do they like each other?" she asked.

"Yeah, their friends. More than that, maybe..."

"Oh, good," said his mother.

Wendy had Randy locked in her vision. She was very relaxed but her eyes betrayed a pure focused determination of a veteran fighter. Randy's eyes shifted from side to side.

"Who is that girl?" Janice asked Adam. "That's not the gentle, loving, daughter that I know. Is this going to get serious?"

"No," he assured her.

Randy slapped out at her a few times. She effortlessly evaded with minimum movement. He suddenly stepped in with a faked left that he followed up with a right hook that looked a bit more serious than Adam was comfortable with. She slapped his left down hard, and raised both forearms in an X formation. She twisted both of her arms, capturing his right. As he spun to the left, she pushed him away with some force. The back of his left hand was red from the slap and he was shaking it out as if to regain feeling to it.

He charged in at her. She smoothly grabbed both of his upper arms and rolled with the attack. They both went down and she sent him sprawling.

When they were both back up facing each other, she

suddenly walked right up to him, stopped with her chest three inches from his. Surprised, he grabbed her, taking hold of her upper body. She seemed to fluidly melt in his arms and slipped out, grabbing both of his arms and twisting them behind his back. He dove forward, freeing himself. Then he charged, swinging. She countered, blocking all of his moves. He continued charging, pushing her back, attempting to overwhelm her with his height and weight. He got in close and threw her in a headlock. She spun in place and kicked his legs out from under him and they both went down.

There followed moves and counter moves which looked more like cage fighting. He would seem to get the advantage with this weight and size and she would fluidly slip out of his control. She spun away, freeing herself. Her shoulders were red when she got to her feet. The last exchange had been serious for them both. When they reached their feet, she charged at him and leaped into the air, locking her legs over his left shoulder and under the right and spun him to the ground. She grabbed his right arm in what looked like a painful hold. As she applied pressure, he struggled desperately.

Adam could see what she was doing and got very concerned.

"Randy, tap out! She's got you! Wendy, be careful! You could break his arm!"

Suddenly Randy twisted so fast he seemed to disappear from one position and reappear in another. He was free of the hold but not free of her grasp.

She reached to throw him in another hold but he slipped out; her momentum had been broken. He rolled to his feet. She tumbled into standing position, facing him.

Adam stood and approached them.

"I'm calling this and declaring a draw! You've both had plenty of time and you were unable to overcome your opponent."

Randy relaxed and extended his hand to Wendy.

"That's not—I was just getting warmed up!" she said turning toward Adam.

"Oh, I'm sure!" Adam said as he turned and walked back to where Janice was sitting.

"Who is that girl?" Janice asked Adam. "What have you done with my daughter?"

"I just made sure that she did what she was doing in the best possible way. I'm not pushing her to fight, just making sure that if she is going to do it, she's going to do it right. And she is. She'll never again be terrorized by guys she bumps into when she's walking home at night."

"Yeah, but she's so..."

"Well, I never expected her to get that good," he said. "That's all her."

"Is she that good with a gun?" she asked.

"She's even better," he said, looking into her eyes.

*　　*　　*

The crowd had finished eating, for the most part and were focusing their attention on the beer and wine.

"You think it's time?" he asked.

She gazed at him emotionally. "They do seem to have a healthy buzz going on."

As he stood, he addressed the crowd with a loud voice. "Could I have everyone's attention? Thank you all for coming. I hope you all enjoyed the ringside entertainment."

The crowd cheered and clapped.s

"I lost ten dollars on that fight!" Joseph yelled.

"That's because you foolishly bet that Randy was going to "kick her butt", which he definitely failed to do," Dawn said. "Serves you right."

"I have an announcement!" Adam said, hesitating. When the crowd was quiet and he had their attention, he continued. "I have asked Janice to be my wife and she's accepted!"

The crowd cheered, clapped and whistled.

"Thank you," said Adam. "And I hope none of you are driving home."

*   *   *

~ 7 ~

Audrey

"What is going on with you?" Janice demanded.

Jenny seemed to shudder. *Nothing,* she mumbled as she looked away.

"No, enough is enough." Janice scolded. "You've been moping around like your best friend just died. But it can't be that because your best friend is—"

I can't talk about it.

"OK," her mother said. "Then you better! What is it?"

Jenny said nothing, but started fading.

"You're not going anywhere, young lady!" her mother snapped. "You get back here!"

Jenny grew more solid on the couch in front of her mother.

"Have you talked to Dolly about whatever it is that's bothering you?"

I can't, Jenny said sadly. *Dolly is what's bothering me.*

Her mother got very attentive. "How is Dolly the problem? Dolly's *never* the problem."

You wouldn't understand...

"That's a bit unfair!" her mother snapped. "What is left that I wouldn't understand?"

She wants to go away...

"Where?" her mother quickly responded. "Where does

she want to go to?"

Jenny started to speak, then hesitated.

You wouldn't understand...

"What?" her mother said, the growing frustration evident in her voice. "I've accepted you; I've accepted Dolly, I've accepted your ghost friends; what's left to understand? Aliens?!"

When she saw her daughter brace herself, she knew she would get her to tell her everything.

Dolly wants to go back...

"To where?"

To be alive...

"What? What do you mean? She is alive! I mean, she's dead, but she's a ghost. Her body died a long time ago, but Dolly is quite alive."

She wants to be alive like our sisters; she wants to have a body. She wants to be alive again.

"Wait a minute! She wants to be alive again? So, everyone can see her?"

Yeah, Jenny snapped angrily. *Maybe she wants to feel what it's like to get hit by a car! Or shot in the chest!*

"That's impossible!" her mother said. "She already lived. And died. What kind of silliness is she getting into? That's just not true!"

That's what I thought, Jenny said. *It is true.*

"You're kidding me! How could she even..."

I guess ghosts do it all the time, Jenny said.

"That's a bit hard to swallow..." her mother said.

Yeah, Jenny said. *Like believing in ghosts...*

"Wow," her mother said. "Just when I think I've heard everything from you two, you come up with something like this!"

Yeah, she claims that I could do it; I could go off and be born as someone's baby somewhere... not that I ever would.

"So, what are you saying? She wants to be a living person again?"

Yes! Jenny said a bit too emphatically. *She wants to leave and go away!*

"What? How? You mean like get born as a baby? How..." She stopped and looked off into space for a moment.

"Dolly! I want to see you right now!"

Dolly appeared beside Jenny, looking a bit guilty. She looked over at Jenny, then at their mother, and then back at Jenny.

What did you say? she demanded angrily. *You promised not to say anything to anyone!*

She's our mother, Jenny said, looking down sadly.

"Dolly, what is going on?" their mother demanded.

I... she hesitated, looking down in a similar fashion. *I was alive for fourteen years. I've been dead for almost two hundred and fifty. I'm just a spectator. I can feel the rain, but not on my skin. I see boys—handsome boys but I can't talk to them! I want that. I can perceive anything; I can permeate anything, but I can't really touch anything. I want to be the smartest girl in school. I want to go to high school dances and slap a boy's hand when he tries to feel me up. I want to feel life on my skin.*

Janice said nothing for a moment, then muttered, "Wow... How is this even possible?"

It happens all the time from what I can see. I've seen people die, then get born again, and decades later they die again, and a couple of years later I see them playing in a playground. There is one ghost in the graveyard who claims to have lived over two dozen times! I know one very clever guy who died and took the fetus his wife was carrying and became his own son. He inherited his own fortune eventually.

"Girls, I've been blindsided by this; I am going to need some time on this one," she said as, shaking her head, she headed for the kitchen.

*   *   *

"So, you're going to just sit here in the open?" Janice asked. "Clearly visible to everyone?"

Why not? Dolly said. *When I get like this, people can't tell.*

Janice was sitting at a table outside a local café. She was going to meet Adam for lunch in an hour, so she decided to relax with a cup of coffee until he showed. Then Dolly and Jenny showed up walking down the sidewalk in her direction. When they reached her, they sat as if they had an appointment.

"How do I explain you to people?" Janice asked. "I know a lot of people in this town!"

Tell them the truth! Dolly said. *I was a close friend of your daughter's.*

"And you," she said, turning to Jenny. "You're not going to pull any funny stuff?"

No! Jenny said. *I'm not visible to anyone else.*

"I guess I should be thankful for that," her mother said, relaxing.

I just want to be with people, Dolly said. *I just want to be as real as I can. I can at least pretend to sit in the sunshine and enjoy the cool breeze, at least for a little bit.*

"I'm too smart for that, Dolly," Janice said. "I know you can feel the breeze. Not on your skin, of course, but you can definitely feel it if you wish."

Yeah, but still... Dolly mumbled.

"Janice?"

They all looked up to see a pretty, dark-haired girl in her late twenties.

"Audrey? Oh, my goodness! It's good to see you again."

The girl turned to Dolly. "Hi, I'm Audrey."

"This is Dolly," Janice said. "She was Jenny's best friend."

"Ooh... that is so sad."

"This is Adam's cousin, Audrey," Janice said to Dolly.

I know Adam quite well. Wendy and I have become best friends; I practically live at their house. Do you want to sit down for a bit? Dolly asked.

Audrey looked at Janice with a quick question in her eyes.

"Sit!" Janice said.

Jenny watched as the three of them chatted amiably. *Dolly is such a character! She simply sits beside Mom, and anyone can see her.* Jenny didn't think she could ever make herself look that solid. But if Adam's cousin looked closely, she could notice things about Dolly...

No, people don't look, she thought to herself.

"So, I hear your oldest is quite a scrapper," Audrey said to Janice.

You heard about that? Dolly asked, surprised.

"Well, yeah," Audrey said. "People have been talking about that fight ever since it happened."

"It wasn't a fight," Janice said. "We don't like to call it that. It was friendly sparring. She's training him to fight 'the right way,' as she calls it. She didn't win the fight—it was a draw. But I think she won a boyfriend."

It never occurred to me to find a boyfriend like that, Dolly said. *Just kick his butt and lead him away by the hand. Wow.*

"It wasn't like that," Janice said.

Dolly just grinned.

*   *   *

Dolly turned to Audrey. *How far along are you?*

"What?" Audrey asked. "What are you—"

Well, I mean... how many weeks? How far along?

"Pregnant? I'm not pregnant! Why would you think that?" she said, quite irritated.

I didn't mean to upset you, Dolly said.

"How would you even know?" Audrey demanded.

I don't know, Dolly stammered. *Sometimes I can just tell...*

"Are you sure?" Janice asked Dolly rather intently.

Dolly hesitated with an uncertain half-smile on her face, then nodded.

Mom, Jenny said, *if Dolly says she's pregnant, she's pregnant.*

"She's pretty good with this kind of thing," Janice said, turning to Audrey. "It gives me chills down my spine. If she said that to me, I would definitely take a test."

Audrey got a concerned look in her eyes. "Now you're freaking me out. How long are you going to be here?" she asked Janice.

"A while. I'm going to meet Adam in 30 minutes. Why?"

"I'll be back in ten," she said and got up.

They watched as she headed down the sidewalk. When she got to the next block, she disappeared into a drugstore.

In ten minutes, she was back. She turned to Dolly and Janice.

"Either you two are pulling the greatest practical joke of all time or..." She reached into the bag she was carrying and pulled out a pregnancy test.

"Don't go anywhere," she said as she turned away from them, "I'll be back,"

"You are such a troublemaker," Janice whispered.

Well, she is! Dolly said as she watched Audrey disappear into the cafe. *She should find out sooner than later.*

"And you stay right here, young lady!" Janice said to Jenny. "You give her privacy."

I wouldn't— she stammered as she looked up to see Adam approaching their table.

Hi! she said.

Janice turned and smiled up at Adam.

"Hi," he said as he took a seat beside Janice.

"Audrey is here." Janice said. "She's in the lady's room; Dolly has caused a bit of an uproar."

"What? How?" Adam asked.

"Didn't you notice how solid Dolly looks today?" Janice asked. "Visible to everyone."

"Oh yes, now that you mention it. Have you been talking to Audrey?"

Well... yes, Dolly said hesitantly.

"Dolly told her that she's pregnant," Janice said.

"I didn't know she was pregnant," Adam said.

"Nobody did," Janice replied. "Dolly discovered it. Right now, she is in the lady's room taking a test."

She's coming, Jenny said.

They all turned to see Audrey coming through the restaurant door.

"Hi, Adam," she said somberly.

She turned to Dolly. "How did you know?" she said seriously.

Dolly shrugged her shoulders. *I don't know. It just comes to me. My grandmother was the same way. She just knew things, somehow.*

Audrey said nothing more, but her eyes focused off in the distance. She turned to Janice.

"I've got to go," she said as she stood, picked up her purse and the bag she had placed on the chair beside her.

"Call me," Janice said. "Anything you need—we're

family now."

"Yeah," she said with a deep sigh. "I've got to let Jarrett know. Wow..."

"It was good to meet you," she said as she turned to Dolly. "I appreciate you letting me know, although you've got me wondering how you knew."

Good luck, Dolly said as Audrey turned and walked away.

Wow, Dolly looked relieved. *For a minute I thought she was going to reach out to take my hand.*

"You take too many risks," Janice said, shaking her head.

Who is Jarrett? Dolly asked.

"He's Audrey's boyfriend," Adam said. "He's been a friend of mine for years. Problem is, he left to go to Pakistan a month ago. Now she's got to track him down. He's special forces. He may not even be in Pakistan."

"He'll be happy, though," Janice said.

And it's a girl, Dolly said.

"So... you're quite sure of this?"

Dolly nodded without taking her attention from the street.

*   *   *

Over the next several months, Dolly monitored Audrey and became familiar with where she lived. Janice was determined to get to know her better as well. She arranged to bump into her often, and they became friends.

Jenny spent a few days moping around, but eventually accepted it. With her mother's help, she decided to just make the best of it.

Janice was sitting at the table outside the café where she regularly met Adam for lunch. She stared in admiration as he appeared a block away, walking toward her.

"Hi," he said as he took a seat across from her. "Wow. No pesky ghosts!"

"Oh hush," she said. "I know how much you love those girls."

"I do!" he said.

"And?" she prompted him to continue.

"I also love my time alone with you. That's tough when you're engaged to seven females who live in the same house."

"What?" She looked confused and then relaxed. "Oh, yeah."

"I have some news," he said.

"Oh?"

"Jarrett has gotten time off to get married. He's flying in tonight. But there's bad news..."

She looked at him, waiting for him to continue.

"He's only got three days off, and then he has to go back."

"Wow," she said. "This is going to be a challenge..."

*   *   *

It was a challenge—but Janice, Adam's mother, Audrey's mother, Wendy, and Dawn worked like a team to pull off the wedding. It was supposed to be a quick affair, with a much larger formal wedding on their first anniversary, when Jarrett would be a civilian. But their quick affair with twelve people somehow became sixty-four. So, they rented a space in a "Bridal Park" overlooking the Atlantic Ocean.

Jenny and Dolly watched the ceremony from a beautiful alder tree. It was a perfect Indian Summer Day in October, and the tree was at the height of its color, with gorgeous red leaves.

They could have had it in the graveyard, Jenny mumbled.

What? Dolly said.

Yeah, that's my favorite place.

Graveyards are for funerals, silly, Dolly insisted. *Not for weddings! Graveyards are where things end, not where they begin.*

Oh, yeah... Jenny said. *You're much too clever for me.*

No, just a bit more common sense, Dolly said. *The wedding is starting. Behave yourself.*

*   *   *

~ 8 ~

Time For Me to Go

"I'm staying away from all of that stuff," Henge said. "I gave that up forever. We both saw what happened in that crypt... I've never been so scared in my life!"

They were sitting on a park bench four blocks from the school.

"What was that thing?" Dawn asked. "It wasn't real, but..."

"It was a demon! We were swimming in the deep end, and we almost drowned..."

"We did that?"

"Yes," Henge said. "We summoned it! I felt like such a stupid, naïve little girl."

"Yeah," Dawn mumbled. "If it wasn't for my sister..."

"Yeah," Henge agreed. "Wendy is pretty badass!"

Dawn missed Henge's misunderstandings. She wasn't listening; she was recalling being crushed by terror, curled up in a fetal position in her bed, feeling her sanity slip away, when Jenny appeared as an angel to save her, to bring her back to something close to reality.

"I want to know what that other thing was, the thing that crushed the demon," Henge said. "I guess for years I've been slipping over to the dark side. I was letting certain people convince me that Satan was the real superhero and all the rest was just a scam."

"What do you mean?" Dawn asked.

"I was convinced that evil was always going to win…"

Dawn stared at her, wondering if she was going to continue.

"But whatever that was that attacked the demon was nothing from the dark side," Henge said. "That was light; there was a goodness about it that the demon couldn't even stand in the presence of."

Dawn knew what that light was; she knew what crushed the demon—it was her stepsister, Dolly, who, ironically, was a very powerful ghost who had been around since the 18th century.

*   *   *

"Mom, there's a cop gonna knock at the front door," Lizzie said.

Janice walked into the living room to find the twins kneeling on the couch, peering through the curtains out the front window. As she opened the door, she recognized the young cop.

"Graham, what's happening?"

"Adam sent me to come get you. He tried to call, but he couldn't get through."

"My phone died. What is happening?"

"Wendy was arrested, but they dropped the charges. Adam wants you to come get the girls."

"What did she do?" Janice demanded.

"Adam said that he would explain everything."

"What was she arrested for?"

"She injured five boys in a fight; two of them are still in the hospital with broken bones."

She gave the cop a stunned look before she spoke. "I'll be there in fifteen minutes."

"I'll let him know," he said as he turned and headed down the steps.

As she closed the door and turned, Jenny and Dolly appeared before her.

In a nutshell, Jenny said. Dawn was with Henge. They met up with Henge's boyfriend, who was a gang member. Two more guys showed up and insisted that they all go to their clubhouse. The guys had been drinking, and things got out of hand. When they started getting physical, the girls tried to leave. Wendy walked in on two of them in an attempted rape on Henge. When she saw that the third had torn Dawn's blouse off, she didn't pull any punches. When two of the gang leaders walked in and saw three of their gang unconscious or injured, they attacked Wendy. The rest is just history.

She didn't put all five in the hospital... Janice said.

No, but she lost it when she saw Dawn half-naked..., Jenny said.

Good! Janice said angrily.

They had history, Dolly added. Three of these guys were the ones that harassed Wendy when we first met.

"How did Wendy find out what was happening and where they were?" Janice said, speaking aloud.

When Jenny reacted, Janice got angry. Dolly stepped

back out of the range of her anger.

"You told her!" Janice exclaimed. "You told her where her sister was and what was happening! You could have handled this! It would have been nothing for the two of you!"

We couldn't; it would have been too visible, Dolly said. *We could have done a lot but how would it have been explained? Henge already has a lousy reputation and Dawn is connected to her. There would have been rumors wild rumors, tearing through the school faster than the speed of light. These two girls would have been ostracized. As it is now, their reputation is that they are no one to mess with.*

Mom, we'll help you out on this, Jenny said. *We'll all get through it.*

"You'll babysit the twins while I go bail out my other two daughters!" she said as she grabbed her purse, passed through the front door, and was gone.

* * *

Janice walked into the living room to find the twins sitting glumly, doing nothing.

"What's happening with you two?" she asked.

"Nothing," Lizzie murmured.

"We're sad," Debbie said.

"Both of you? Why?"

"Cause Jenny's sad," Debbie said.

"Jenny? What are you talking about?"

"She's sad," Lizzie said.

"When do you—how do you..., how do you know

Jenny is sad?"

"She's a ghost," Debbie said nonchalantly. "We see her all the time. And that other girl, Dolly. She's a ghost too."

"You see them?"

"Yeah. Late at night, mostly."

"How long have you been seeing them?"

"Long time," Lizzie said.

"Does she come in your room?" Janice asked.

"Sometimes," Lizzie said. "But it's OK."

"She's sad?" Janice asked. "Why?"

"I don't know," Lizzie said. "I think she's sad about Dolly. Dolly's her best friend."

Wow, Janice thought to herself. *They know. And it seems that it's nothing out of the ordinary to them. Wonders never cease with my girls.*

*   *   *

Where have you been? Jenny asked.

With Audrey... Dolly said. *I just—I just want to make sure nothing happens.*

She'll be fine, Jenny said sourly.

Things had become strained between the two ghosts.

Listen, Dolly said. *We have been through a lot—your accident, your coma, your death. But we've always been good. I love you more than anyone, and we're going to be best friends forever.*

Yeah, Jenny said, staring off. *It's just...*

I know, Dolly said. *And I've probably made it worse by spending so much time around Audrey. I will spend the rest of my time with you. I'll just let her be. You're right. She'll be OK; nothing's going to happen.*

Jenny nodded with an attempted smile as Dolly surrounded and embraced her.

*   *   *

"She seems very healthy," Janice said.

She was in the living room with Dolly, Jenny, and Wendy. Wendy was reading one of Adam's gun magazines and wasn't paying much attention to the conversation.

"You have a daddy now," Janice continued.

Yes, Dolly said. *It would be inappropriate to be born out of wedlock.*

After a moment, Janice spoke. "She has good hips."

What? Jenny asked. *What does that have to do with anything? Sounds like something construction workers might say when she walks by the construction job: 'Hey Joe, look at the hips on that babe!'* she said, imitating a rough man's voice.

"You're certainly on edge," Janice said. "It means she'll have an easy delivery. I wish I had hips like that. All five deliveries would have been much easier."

Oh, Dolly said. *I see.*

Jenny said nothing.

"This is a beautiful gun," Wendy said.

What? said Jenny, wondering what Wendy could possibly be talking about.

"Yeah... it's a Sig Sauer P365. 9-millimeter. Beautiful gun."

You need another gun? Dolly asked.

"Yeah," Wendy said wistfully. "But that Smith & Wesson Shield is nice too."

Yeah, you could really shoot a lot of people with that sucker, said Dolly, sounding completely out of character.

Why do you need another gun? Jenny asked. *You're dangerous enough without a gun.*

"I have a .22 caliber semi-automatic. It's a girl's gun."

Oh, said Dolly. *We can't have that...*

"With taxes, I'll probably end up spending $500. I bet I could sweet-talk Adam..."

"You need to find a better way," said Janice. "Maybe Christmas or something. Don't be hitting my man up for cash!" Janice said in a silly accent.

"Hmmm, you guys wouldn't understand," she said as she stood. "I've got to meet Randy in 20 minutes."

What's happening? Jenny asked.

"Nothing, we're just going to hang out," she said.

Are you going to keep him? Jenny asked.

"Yeah," she said. "I think so."

Of course, Dolly said. *You weren't able to defeat him, so now...*

"Oh?" said Wendy. "So that's why? No. He is one guy I will never have to defend in a fight. All the others are too fragile. I think he's almost unbreakable."

"Yes, you sorely tested that point," Janice said.

*   *   *

There was caution in Dolly's voice as she turned to Jenny.

We need to talk.

Jenny looked at her mother and realized that whatever she wanted to discuss, she and Janice had already started the conversation.

It's time for me to go.

Jenny said nothing but sat stiffly looking at Dolly.

"She does," Janice said. "If she's going to do this, she needs to go now."

I don't want any emotional goodbyes, Dolly said. *At the most, I'll only be gone for a couple of years; you'll find me. I have already talked to Wendy.*

Jenny hesitated, then spoke.

I can't cry anymore. I guess I'll just wait for you. I will watch over you when you are a toddler, and I'll always be around for you. I'll be easy to find...

She hesitated, suppressing a bit of grief. *Just look over your right shoulder...*

I love you both so much, Dolly said. And she was gone.

*   *   *

"Dolly's gone...," Adam said. "I am going to miss her quite a bit. I haven't known her that long, and I was just beginning to accept her as my daughter. It never occurred to me that it would hit me as such a loss, but it does."

"Because it's Dolly," Janice said.

They sat quietly for a few moments, saying nothing.

"How are you doing?" Adam asked.

She said nothing for a moment. "It hurts. Actually, I'm devastated. It stirs up all those terrible feelings I had when

Jenny died."

"How is Jenny doing?" he asked.

"Better than I thought. She has been with the twins ever since Dolly left. And the girls are thrilled to get all this attention. She plays all of their imaginary games with them and helps them with their schoolwork. It is a blessing for all three of them."

"Nice," he said.

*   *   *

~ 9 ~

Ghosts and Souls

"We talked about this and we decided to let you be our best friend," Lizzie said.

"Yeah," Debbie agreed. "We like having a ghost friend and we'll never tell."

I'm already your sister, Jenny said.

"Yeah," Lizzie said, "but not all sisters are friends. We can be both."

I would like that, Jenny said, very much. Are Wendy and Dawn your friends?

"Of course," said Lizzie.

"So," Debbie started, "what's a ghost?"

A ghost is a person, said Jenny, *but without a body.*

"How can a person not have a body?" asked Lizzie.

Am I a person? Jenny asked.

"Of course!" Debbie insisted. "Ghosts are people, too."

Where's my body?

"Ohhh..." Debbie said, while Lizzie just sat and stared.

Well, people don't have a soul, Jenny said. *They have a body, but they are a soul.*

"I don't have a soul?" Lizzie asked.

Can a horse have a horse? Jenny asked. *Can a car have a car?*

"No, silly!" Lizzie said. "A horse can't have a horse! A

horse *is* a horse!"

"Of course, of course," Debbie said in a giggling singsong voice.

"I knew you were going to say that," Lizzie said.

"Of course, of course," Debbie said with a giggling shrug. "You're my twin sister."

OK, so do you have a soul? Jenny asked.

Lizzie sat for a moment, thinking...

"No..., I guess. Because I am a soul."

"Yes," Debbie said. "You are a soul and I am a soul."

"But I'm a little girl," mused Lizzie.

I think you're a soul with a little girl body, Jenny said. *I was a soul with a girl body once, but my body died. Now I'm just a ghost. A soul is a ghost, Jenny said. A ghost is a soul.*

Debbie suddenly brightened up. Jenny could see her mind working.

*   *   *

Dolly watched as Audrey grabbed a towel and stepped out of the shower. She dried herself off, then wrapped a second towel around her hair. She walked into the bedroom and carefully slipped on her nightgown, taking care to get it over the towel. Dolly's attention was fixated on Audrey's enormous stomach and large breasts.

So, she's going to be my mommy. I'm going to be a baby, then a little girl, then a teenager like Jenny was...

She thought of going to school, of playing in the snow, of walking in the sunshine on a beautiful day. *And all of the advancements that have been made since I was a girl.*

I'm getting a bit giddy, she thought, *but I will have long hair, maybe blonde or even black. Whatever it is, it will be beautiful. I'm going to be a girl! A real girl! Now I know how Pinocchio felt,* she said to herself, laughing at her own silliness.

Audrey lay on the bed, picked up a remote and turned on the TV. Dolly settled on Audrey's stomach, feeling its warmth and slight moisture from the shower.

She reached out to embrace; there was a click as she took possession of the fetus. And then nothing.

*   *   *

"I'm a ghost, Mommy."

"You're a what?" Janice asked Lizzie.

"I'm a ghost! Debbie's a ghost, too!"

"Jenny's a ghost. You're a little girl. Who told you that?"

"Jenny."

"So, you're the same as Jenny? When did you die?"

"I didn't. I'm a ghost with a body."

"Yes, technically you're a ghost. But when a ghost has a body, they call that a soul. You're a soul with a body."

"Yes," Lizzie said. "A ghost."

"I guess you can be called a ghost if you want to be," Janice said.

*   *   *

"Jenny!" Janice called. She was standing in Jenny's space off the dining room. Jenny appeared beside her.

"What did you do?" she asked angrily.

257

What do you mean?

"What did you tell your little sisters?"

Jenny was stunned by her mother's upset. *I-I felt that I had to explain—* Jenny was stumbling with her words.

"I know what you said to them, but you did a half a job! That was going to be Lizzie's next show-and-tell, all this about souls and ghosts and babies and bodies. They couldn't wait to tell all their friends!"

Oh, my God, Jenny said. *I didn't think...*

"You certainly didn't. I had to spend quite a bit of time with them explaining why they would have to keep that to themselves, how other people wouldn't understand and how many problems it would cause for them to talk about this!"

I'm sorry... I am so sorry. That was so stupid of me!

"You know how those two are. I had to explain to them about different religions and different beliefs and how crazy people can get with the subject of religion. I want to raise them so that they can talk to anybody about any-thing, but with this..."

Oh no! I will talk with them; I will spend time with them and make it OK. I will make this good. I can't handle you being angry with me.

"Then make this go away."

I will, Jenny said.

*   *   *

~ 10 ~

Living and Dying

Janice watched through the front window as Adam pulled his pickup into the driveway and got out. *I am so happy with this man;* she thought as she walked to the kitchen to greet him at the door when he came in.

"Hi," she said as she reached out to embrace him. "Supper will be ready in about thirty minutes."

As she looked into his eyes, she saw sorrow, stress, and concern. *Oh crap!* she said to herself.

"What's happened?" she asked.

"Give me a moment," he said as he reached in the refrigerator and grabbed a bottle of beer. She followed him into the living room. When he settled into his recliner, she sat on the couch and turned toward him.

"What?" she asked.

"Jarrett's dead. His Hummer ran over an IED; killed him and one other soldier, injured three others."

"Oh no!" Janice was stunned. "Does Audrey know?"

"They just left her house."

"Wendy! Dawn!" The two girls entered the living room as she stood.

"I need you to take care of supper and the twins; I've got to go." She grabbed her purse and disappeared out the front door.

*　　*　　*

Dolly had a dim awareness of darkness, of fluid, of float-ing of noises, squeaks and burps, a stomach growling; of pressure digestion, bowel movements, cramps and bend-ing over; of impact bumping into something, often. She had a dim vision of her mother. She reached toward this bond developing between them. She reveled in the grow-ing love, the developing intimacy. She didn't know where she was or who she was all she knew was the security of this intimacy with the woman who was her whole world.

*　　*　　*

Jenny watched Adam, Janice, and Audrey as they stood in the bright sun and biting winds of a November morning as the flag-draped coffin was unloaded from the huge C130 military aircraft. She had an acute awareness of the suffer-ing and the sorrow that *Dolly's* mother was experiencing, and to a lesser degree, Janice and Adam.

Oh Dolly, what will come of all this?

The bewildered ghost watched as the *line* of black lim-ousines followed the military escort out of the circular drive of the funeral home to the cemetery. He watched as they lowered the coffin into the ground, followed by the sa-lute of the guns. He saddened as people started dispersing.

Jarrett? How are you doing? Jenny asked.

Who are you? he wondered.

I'm Janice's oldest daughter. Do you remember the school shooting a few years ago at Thayer?

You're her...

Yes, she said.

What now? he asked.

What do you want? she asked.

I don't know, he said sadly. *I really loved her; I still love her. I wanted to have a family. I tried to do everything right but now...*

You can go back... Jenny said softly.

What? he asked.

I don't mean back I mean you can go find a baby body, maybe at a hospital, and be born into another life. Or you can just hang around and become a loiterer like me, she said bitterly.

He seemed lost as he glanced at her. *Yes, I want that.*

Which? I gave you two choices.

I want to go back. I want to be born into a family.

Go find a maternity ward, she said. *Don't give it much thought. Just decide that is what you are going to do, and I think the rest will take care of itself.*

He looked at her thoughtfully and then said, *thank you, I'll do that.*

Oh yeah don't try to take the body of the child your wife is carrying! That's already taken!

Yeah, he said sadly. *That's probably best.*

*   *   *

"I don't know what to do," Janice said. "She is crippled by this. I am concerned with her and with Dolly. She needs help."

"She will be seeing counselors at the base—loss counselors as well as pregnancy counselors," Adam said. "I know this is hard, but I think we should refer to her as 'Audrey's baby.' She is not our Dolly anymore. When she is born, she'll have a different name."

Janice nodded sadly as Jenny appeared beside her. *How are you doing?*

She looked at Jenny before her glance settled on the floor in front of her.

"I think that I need to sit down and cry for about an hour, and then I'll be all right. Do you know how Dolly is?"

No; I have no contact with her. I'll keep trying...

*   *   *

"Tomorrow then," Janice said as she left Audrey's hospital room.

As she started down the corridor, Jenny was beside her.

How far along is she now?

Seven months, Janice said.

How is she doing?

I don't really know, Janice said slowly. *Sometimes I wonder if she even wants to live. Other times, I just don't know. Her whole world collapsed in one crushing moment.*

I could go and... Jenny said.

No! Janice insisted. *I don't think it's a good idea to go anywhere near her, especially since you can't even reach Dolly.*

I feel for her, Jenny said. *I feel helpless, lost, and lonely and I'm not even the one involved in this. I...*

Janice glanced over at her daughter.

I just think of Dolly...

I think of nothing else, Janice said.

*   *   *

Dolly was startled as everything seemed to be in motion. She got a vision of a gurney and the movement of people. A relaxing, almost intoxicating sensation washed over her, and she was floating.

Suddenly, a sharp tearing pain pierced the side of her face. The pain continued as it tore down through her face and into her chest. Something crushed against the side of her head as it was forced over. She was wrenched into a soundless, endless scream.

Something clamped onto her leg and she was violently twisted as both of her legs were pulled into the wet cold... She was overwhelmed by a shock of pain that stabbed into the back of her neck, into her spine, and continued down further into her flesh.

Burning fire ripped through her as something bit deep into her shoulder. She seemed to be writhing in a crashing surf of scalding white fire as an arm that was no longer hers was torn from her body. As something stabbed into the other side of her face, her other arm was in a crushing grip.

She had no resistance to the searing, separating pain that effortlessly overwhelmed and controlled everything. There was no acceptance, rejection, or tolerance as it all flared into a nothingness as she was torn from the flesh; it was no longer her flesh as she was jerked into a voracious darkness that swallowed everything.

*   *   *

It's me and you, girl, Janice said. *At least for a while.*

I don't know what I would do if I didn't have you, Jenny said.

She'll be back. It may take her a while, but you two always find each other. When you were hit by the car, she found you. When you came home from the hospital, she found you. It took a while, but you two are always back together.

Yeah, Jenny said.

Spend some time with your sisters. The twins are wondrously fascinated with you; Dawn is still a bit lost and could use a friend. And Wendy you know Wendy she definitely needs a guiding hand. Adam tries, but I think she has him in the palm of her hand...

Suddenly, the front door burst open and Adam's bulk was a dark silhouette against the afternoon light. Then he was standing in the center of the living room; his face was red; his fists were clenched and he was shaking; it was obvious that he was in a rage.

"What is going on?" Janice demanded.

"That slutty little piece of garbage! Cowardly piece of trash! I would rather have him dead than see this!"

"What has happened?!!" Janice said, grabbing onto both of his arms.

"She killed her! That—she doesn't deserve to live! I'm glad he's gone!"

"Who killed who?" Janice demanded.

"Audrey! She killed Dolly!"

"What? What do you mean?"

"She—she aborted—she got rid of the baby! She killed Dolly!"

Janice reeled as if she had been slapped, hard. Her hand went to her mouth and she stumbled backward. Adam reached forward to keep her from falling.

"No, no! That's not true! She couldn't have!"

Suddenly Jenny was in front of both of them.

Sit! she insisted. *We need to talk urgently!*

This is going to be all right, Jenny said. *She destroyed Dolly's flesh, but she will survive this, and I will find her!*

They sat on the couch; their desperate glances locked on Jenny.

"Do we need to hide Wendy's guns?" Adam asked.

No, Jenny said angrily. *Do I need to hide yours?*

Adam looked down as he shook his head.

This is going to be OK, Jenny said. *The flesh was destroyed and I'm sure it was a devastatingly traumatic event for Dolly, but I will find her and bring her back. But I need both of you to pull yourselves together and put our home back on a normal course. Neither Dawn nor the twins need to know anything about this. I will find Wendy and tell her and ensure she will be OK, but then I won't be back until I find Dolly.*

She disappeared.

*　　　*　　　*

~ 11 ~

Into the Future

Two weeks later Jenny was in a deep cave in the White Mountains of New Hampshire. She probed below the rather large boulder.

Hey, she said.

Nothing.

Hey, she repeated.

Dolly just bristled.

Hey, demon slayer.

What? Dolly spat out.

I need you to do something for me; I need your help.

What?

You have to come out before I can tell you.

Jenny waited, listening to Dolly think about what she said.

How far?

Oh, far, Jenny said.

What? Dolly said, appearing as a vague figure.

I'll be waiting outside the cave for you. It's a nice day out.

Ten minutes later, Dolly appeared at the cave entrance where Jenny waited.

Not very solid, Jenny said.

What do you need?

An oak tree, said Jenny.

An oak tree? demanded Dolly. *Are you crazy?*

An oak tree.

Right there in front of you! Dolly snapped.

Where? asked Jenny.

There! she said, pointing.

Good, said Jenny.

I need a creek... said Jenny emphatically.

Why? asked Dolly.

I need a creek, said Jenny.

Follow me, said Dolly.

A moment later they hovered above a creek.

Is that all? demanded Dolly.

I've never seen a moose. I need a moose.

Come on! Dolly growled.

Twenty minutes later Jenny was still instructing Dolly.

A boulder? Why do you need a boulder?

A big boulder, Jenny insisted, *the biggest one you can find.*

Look! Right here! Do you see that boulder? That is the biggest boulder you will find anywhere! I guarantee you won't find a bigger boulder!

That's what I wanted!

Dolly looked at her suspiciously.

I need a mountain! That's what I need, a mountain.

You're standing on one!

Where? Show me!

Look! Across that huge valley. A mountain!

Yes! Jenny said.

Anything else? demanded Dolly.

Yes, Jenny said. *Vermont!*

Vermont?!

Yes, Jenny repeated. *I need Vermont. It must be around here somewhere.*

Come with me, Dolly said.

Jenny followed her several thousand feet into the air.

There! Dolly said, pointing.

Where?

You see that ridge, way over there?

Jenny nodded.

Everything on the other side of that ridge is Vermont. Everything south of that and north of that, that you can see, is Vermont.

I have Vermont, Jenny said.

Dolly started to say something but stopped.

What? Jenny asked.

Dolly hesitated. *You!*

What?

You didn't even ask me how I was.

That was inconsiderate of me, Jenny said. *How are you?*

I'm fine! Dolly said with a hint of frustration.

Where have you been?

Dolly pointed toward the cave.

Where are you now? Jenny asked.

I'm right here! You can't tell where I am? I'm right in front of you.

Is this better than that?

Dolly looked at the sky above them; her gaze dropped

slowly to where she was studying the horizon.

Yes, Dolly said, *look at the mountains; as they stretch off into the distance, each layer becomes a lighter blue.*

Look at those clouds! Jenny exclaimed.

Yes, they're beautiful.

Let's go home, Jenny said.

She looked at Jenny earnestly; a moment later, she nodded.

*   *   *

Life continued for the family. With everyone's help, Dolly left the trauma behind. Assisting with Dolly's healing, Adam left his rage and upset behind.

Dawn, having experienced both sides of the spiritual realm, Dawn attached herself to her sister and ghost, both of the ghosts, actually, and set her sights on college.

Wendy got her driver's license. Janice had uneasy thoughts of manipulation as somehow, Wendy ended up with Adam's pickup truck when he somehow decided he needed a new one, but she let it go. Wendy was acquiring an impressive list of trophies and titles in both her martial arts and marksmanship, and was quietly developing her own, rather spiritual martial arts style. Dawn had been Wendy's first student and was making good progress.

Six months later, the date for their mother's wedding grew near. Janice's father had flown in from California and spent most of the time with his grandchildren.

*   *   *

The weather was most appropriate; bold, detailed clouds were scattered across the sky, creating the perfect diffusion of sunlight. The temperature was 71 degrees. Perfect.

Below them, Adam stood at the front of the nave, waiting proudly. Beside him stood his best man, a huge man, bigger than Adam, dressed in military uniform.

They watched as Janice, walking with her arm linked into her father's, slowly passed down the aisle.

Then came the four bridesmaids Wendy, Dawn and Adam's two sisters.

My gosh, Wendy is beautiful!

Yes, Jenny replied, *incredibly feminine! You'd never guess her secret identity as a human weapon.*

Dawn is getting prettier all the time.

Yes, Jenny said, *she was a late bloomer but she's getting there.*

Behind them strutted the twins, flower girls, both.

Look at those two! Jenny said.

They have such attitude! Dolly said. *Where do they get that?*

I figured it out a while back, Jenny said, *it's very simple; Lizzie gets it from Debbie and Debbie gets it from Lizzie. It's a perpetual attitude machine.*

They watched the twins follow the procession, strutting like two little princesses condescending for the benefit of their subjects.

You gotta give it to them, Jenny said, *they've got the walk down perfect.*

Their thoughts grew silent as Janice reached Adam. Wendy and Dawn joined her as her father backed away.

As the minister's voice droned, Jenny drifted off into prior days. She thought of her early days in the grave-yard when she first met Malcolm and the rest of her ghost friends; to the death of Jeremy and her special friendship with Dolly; to her time in a coma.

She thought of how she had cheated the coma, how she had tumbled off into a mystical playland with the perfect friend. She recalled her struggle to reach through death's darkness to once again embrace her mother.

She thought of Thaddeus, wondering how she had come to be blessed with such people in her life. She recalled how her schooldays ended with two bullets in the chest—only to once again, with Dolly's help, return to her mother.

As her thoughts returned to the present, to the church, to the marriage between her mother and her friend who she had grown to love, the church erupted into cheers.

*   *   *

Oh my god! Jenny gasped to herself. She found that she was unable to move or release herself from the idea that had locked her in its iron grip.

Dolly... she gasped.

What?

Look! Look at the fetus!

Wow! Mom is pregnant? Dolly said. *It didn't take Adam long at all!*

Look at the fetus!

It's not a fetus, Dolly said, *It's two of them!*

Look again! Jenny insisted as she tumbled into tears.

Oh my god! Two more little girls in the family! That's seven! No, it's eight with me!

Hey, you're crying... Dolly hesitated, not knowing what to say. *I don't know why you're crying... What are you upset about?*

I'm not upset... at all!

Suddenly Dolly got it.

No! No, no, no! I know what happens with little girl's bodies in the womb! You get ripped apart! You can't even scream as they tear your little arms off!

*   *   *

Dolly assumed a stillness, a quiescence that Jenny did not know how to respond to. Jenny reached out to permeate her best friend. As she found the space that Dolly had assumed, she found herself sharing something they had never attained before.

She was in an almost full, mutual permeation with Dolly. She was *being* Dolly, and she knew that it was reciprocal—Dolly was being her. She found herself commanding a mutually-created mind—a symbiotic creation that the two of them could maintain for the next few seconds or for an eternity if they wished, as they could be themselves or each other or the common being they had created, for now or forever, if they so desired.

They probed and thought, aligned and evaluated.

They saw the bullets rip through Jenny's body as she died; they saw an uncaring physician tearing Dolly's body apart. They looked at a future where two strangers were born to their mother and Adam and grew up as two more girls in the family. Then they looked at a different future where they lay embraced in the serenity and security of amniotic fluid, only to be interrupted by a cold, wet, noisy birth.

They looked at Jenny's thoughts *I can be her daughter again! I can get back the life that was torn from me!*

They looked at Dolly's thoughts of once again gaining life, this time in the safety and security of one they loved the most *She can be our mother; we can be sisters!*

In the midst of doubts, fears, and anxiety, a decision was made.

*   *   *

The twins were crawling over Adam, part of their daily ritual of trying to physically best him, when the two ghosts appeared.

We need to talk, Jenny said.

Adam turned to his wife. "Something happened; they're both freaked out."

The twins climbed off of Adam and quietly blended into the background, going into their surveillance mode, where their voices were still and their ears were big.

We're not freaked out Jenny said, *we're... Yeah, we're*

freaked out...

Where's Wendy? Dolly asked. *Where's Dawn?*

"What is happening?" Adam asked. "Is this a family meeting of some sort?"

Jenny looked at Dolly. It was a moment before she turned to look back at Adam, then at Janice.

You're pregnant, Jenny said.

"What?" Janice asked. "Are you sure?"

Jenny nodded solemnly.

"Is there a problem? Is the fetus, OK?"

It's OK, but it's not a fetus, it's an embryo, Dolly said.

"What's the difference?" Adam asked.

An embryo becomes a fetus at eight weeks.

"And?" Janice asked impatiently.

Jenny looked over to Dolly again.

"What is going on," Janice demanded. "You're upsetting me!"

I don't mean to! Jenny said. *It's just that...*

It's two embryos! Dolly interrupted. *And they're females!*

"I'm going to have twins again?" Janice said. "Two more girls?"

Jenny and Dolly both nodded slowly.

"That's OK," Adam said, turning to Janice. "I love the girls you have, and the girls you will have will only make me happier."

"Why are they not happy?" Janice demanded, pointing to Jenny and Dolly.

"I don't know," said Adam, turning to the two girls.

They said nothing but just stared intently at Janice.

We're not unhappy. This is difficult for us, Dolly said. *We have struggled with this for a while.*

"What?" she asked as they said nothing.

She got a very concerned look on her face and returned their stare. After a moment, a look of shock lit up her face. Tears burst from her eyes.

"Oh my god! Yes! Please! I want this more than anything!"

Adam stared at the three, quite dumbfounded. "Want what?"

It's... a big decision for us, Jenny said, *a huge decision. We have struggled with this...*

"What?" he demanded. "Now I'm getting upset! Will someone tell me what is going on?"

As Jenny turned to her mother, Dolly turned to handle Adam's irritation.

Adam, listen, said Dolly. *Two female embryos which will soon become two female fetuses.*

"Yeah..." he said, focusing on Dolly.

Two ghosts, she said, pointing toward herself and Jenny.

"Yeah?" he said. A moment later a shock came across his face. "Oh hell! You can do that?"

Yes, Dolly said, *but it's a big decision. It changes everything.*

"I guess! But your mother really wants that...," Adam said, with an intensity spreading across his face, "as do I."

They heard the back door open; a moment later Wendy walked into the room.

"What's going on?" she asked. "The air is thick with..., whatever."

Perceptive, Dolly said.

Dawn appeared at Wendy's side.

"What's going on?" she asked.

"I don't know," Wendy said, "but we just walked in on something."

"I'm pregnant."

"Wow," Wendy said.

"Can you have a little boy this time?" Dawn demanded. "I want a little brother!"

"No," Janice said. "Too late."

"Another girl?" Wendy asked. "My goodness; enough is enough! I thought after you had me..."

"Shut up," Dawn said, punching Wendy's arm, being the only one who could do that and get away with it. "You don't love the twins? I want an answer, 'because I'll tell them!"

"Oh, knock it off," Wendy scolded. "I was teasing you!"

"It's not a little girl," Adam said.

"It's two little girls," Janice said.

"Mom, you're a freak!" Wendy said. "Another set of twins!"

"There go my hopes for a little brother!" Dawn snapped.

"We'll have to think up names!" Wendy said. "That'll be fun."

Well, Jenny said, *one of them will be named Dolly.*

"Why?" Wendy asked.

"That's stupid!" Dawn said frustratedly. "It's a pretty

name, but that name is already taken."

"You continue to make no sense," Wendy said. "What will you name the other?"

Janice, Adam, Jenny and Dolly all exchanged glances before Janice spoke.

"I'm thinking it should be Jenny."

"What?" demanded Dawn.

"Why?" demanded Wendy.

"Oh, I get it!" Debbie said as the twins seemed to suddenly appear from nowhere.

"I like that!" Lizzie said. "That will be so good!"

"You will have two more baby sisters," Janice said. "Do you know who they will be?"

"How would we know?!" Dawn said. "I'm in a house full of crazy people!"

"It's gonna be Dolly and Jenny!" Lizzie said, frustratedly tapping Wendy on the arm.

"Yeah!" Debbie said.

"These two," Adam said, pointing to Jenny and Dolly.

"Well yeah; they're going to have the same name, but—" Wendy stopped. "Oh! Oh my god!" she gasped. "Can you do that?"

Yes! Jenny said, *no question.*

"I think I'll go find another demon," Dawn mumbled.

"What?!" her mother snapped.

"She'll probably make more sense than you guys..." she said.

"Don't even kid about that!" her mother scolded as she pulled Dawn into her lap. "Are you confused?" she asked.

Dawn nodded her head while staring into her mother's face.

"It's gonna be Dolly and Jenny!" Debbie shouted at Dawn, gesturing with both hands.

"Don't you get it?" Lizzie demanded loudly.

"What do you know about Jenny and Dolly?" their mother asked.

"They're ghosts."

"Yes," she replied. "And what is a ghost?"

"Someone who died," Dawn said.

"Yes, but it's a soul, a spirit, whatever."

Dawn nodded.

"OK," Janice said. "I'm just going to be straight out about this. A ghost can possess an unborn baby's body and live again."

"Whoa," Dawn said. "Really?"

"Yes. That's what ghosts do. They die, they're ghosts, they get another body and get born again."

"Oh...," Dawn said, staring off into space. "Really?"

Yes, Dolly said.

"I guess... that kind of makes sense...," Dawn whispered. "In a way."

Jenny and I... Dolly said.

"Yeah?" Dawn asked.

We want to be those two little girl babies in mommy's womb and get born as twins.

"Really?"

"Yeah," said Janice. "They will be our babies; they will be your baby sisters."

"They can do that?"

"Yes."

"What about the two ghosts who were going to be those babies?" asked Dawn.

First come, first served, said Jenny.

Yes, Dolly said. *They're our bodies.*

"You'll be the same girls?"

Oh yes, Jenny said. *We'll even have the same names!*

There was silence as Dawn stared off into space.

"Wow...," she said as something seemed to click. She looked up into her mother's face.

"That's a good idea. Funny how everything works out; we get Jenny back as a real person and Dolly will be our baby sister; they both will. That will be so good!"

"Yeah," said Wendy. "And they get to be sisters, which they're going to love."

"Wow," said Dawn. "The twins will be their big sisters."

"We got this," Debbie insisted, nodding her head as she glanced at her twin.

"Nothing that Jenny and Dolly can't handle," Janice said.

The End

Epilogue

The Dubious Daily Press
Sunday, 24 March 2002

Twin Girls Born to Mother of Slain Student and Police Officer Involved in School Shooting

Two years ago, in a tragic and suicidal attack, Jason Albart and Bobby Bandar entered Thaddeus Thayer Middle School armed with rifles and handguns, intent on killing as many students, teachers, and staff as possible.

One heroic student, Jennifer Jeffries, confronted the shooters in an attempt to dissuade Jason her childhood friend from perpetrating the horrific act. When his partner, Bobby, shot and killed the girl, Jason turned his weapon on Bobby and killed him.

The school police officer, Adam McArthur, then fatally shot Jason, ending the incident.

Local law enforcement officials stated that the brave actions of the young girl helped keep the loss of life to a minimum.

One year ago, Officer McArthur married Janice Jeffries, mother of the slain heroic student. Last week, twin girls were born to Adam and Janice McArthur.

Jennifer is survived by six younger sisters: 15-year-old Wendy, 14-year-old Dawn, 10-year-old twins Deborah and

Elizabeth, and the newborn twin girls.

*   *   *

Characters in this trilogy

Adam McArthur	Security guard at Jenny's school
(Aunt) Agnes	Jenny's anti-social aunt
Amber	Teenage cemetery ghost, Willow's sister
Audrey	Adam's cousin, Dolly's perspective mom
Bobby Bandar	Jason's sidekick, psycho druggie
Brenda	One of Adam's sisters
Chatan Farplain	Jenny's tutor, physical therapist
(The) Creepy guy	Child stalker/pervert who killed Jeremy
Dawn Jeffries	Jenny's 2nd younger sister
Debbie	Jenny's younger sister, one of the twins
Dolly	Jenny's best friend (a ghost).
Eddie	Sidekick to Jeremy, the bully
Henge (Stonehenge)	Dawn's friend, strong interest in the occult
Helen	Adam's mother
Janice Jeffries	Jenny's mother
Jarrett	Audrey's husband, Adam's friend
Jarred	Purse snatcher
Jason Albart	Jenny's childhood friend, psycho druggie
Jenny Jeffries	The main character
Jeremy	Bully who would Harass Jenny
(Sgt) John Remington	Ghost-soldier from WW1
Joseph	Randy's best friend
Julie	A friend of Wendy's at the dojo.
Lady Marie	Ghost-actress at the cemetery

Lance	Ghost-One of the dancers in the park
(Mrs.) Lewiston	Jenny's history teacher
Lizzie	Jenny's younger sister, one of the twins
Malcolm	Ghost-black railroad worker
Mara	Adam's youngest sister, away at college.
Margaret	Ghost-One of the dancers in the park
Martha	Jenny's neighbor, friend of Janice.
Millie	Cemetery ghost too afraid to show herself
Mortimer	Cemetery ghost-actor, play director
Randy	Adam's cousin, Wendy's boyfriend
Sammy (Samuel)	Purse snatcher
Seth	Adam's brother
Thaddeus P Thayer	Ghost, Historical figure, Jenny's mentor
Wendy Jeffries	Janice's 2nd daughter, guns, martial arts
Willow	Teenage cemetery ghost, Amber's sister